Books by Leslie Meier

MISTLETOE MURDER

TIPPY TOE MURDER

TRICK OR TREAT MURDER

BACK TO SCHOOL MURDER

VALENTINE MURDER

CHRISTMAS COOKIE MURDER

TURKEY DAY MURDER

WEDDING DAY MURDER

BIRTHDAY PARTY MURDER

FATHER'S DAY MURDER

STAR SPANGLED MURDER

NEW YEAR'S EVE MURDER

BAKE SALE MURDER

CANDY CANE MURDER

ST. PATRICK'S DAY MURDER

MOTHER'S DAY MURDER

WICKED WITCH MURDER

GINGERBREAD COOKIE MURDER

ENGLISH TEA MURDER

CHOCOLATE COVERED MURDER

EASTER BUNNY MURDER

CHRISTMAS CAROL MURDER

FRENCH PASTRY MURDER

CANDY CORN MURDER

BRITISH MANOR MURDER

EGGNOG MURDER

TURKEY TROT MURDER

SILVER ANNIVERSARY MURDER

YULE LOG MURDER

Published by Kensington Publishing Corporation

ST. PATRICK'S DAY MURDER

LESLIE MEIER

KENSINGTON BOOKS
www.kensingtonbooks.com

KENSINGTON BOOKS are published by

Kensington Publishing Corp.
119 W. 40th Street
New York, NY 10018

All Kensington titles, imprints, and distributed lines are available at special quantity discounts for bulk purchases for sales promotion, premiums, fundraising, educational, or institutional use.

Special book excerpts or customized printings can also be created to fit specific needs. For details, write or phone the office of the Kensington Sales Manager: Attn. Sales Department. Kensington Publishing Corp., 119 W. 40th Street, New York, NY 10018. Phone: 1-800-221-2647.

Kensington and the K logo Reg. U.S. Pat. & TM Off.

First Kensington Hardcover Edition: January 2008

ISBN-13: 978-0-7582-2967-0 (ebook)
ISBN-10: 0-7582-2967-4 (ebook)

ISBN-13: 978-1-4967-2474-8
ISBN-10: 1-4967-2474-7
First Kensington Trade Paperback Edition: February 2019

10 9 8 7 6 5 4 3 2 1

Printed in the United States of America

For Kevin and Beryl Daley

Acknowledgments

Much thanks to Joyce Flynn and Phil O'Leary

Prologue

The last customer hadn't left the bar until nearly two a.m.—well past the eleven p.m. closing time mandated by the town bylaws in Tinker's Cove, Maine—but that didn't bother Old Dan very much. He'd never been one to fuss about rules and regulations. No, he was one who took the inch and made it a mile. If they wanted him to close at eleven, well, they could jolly well send over a cop or two or ten and make him. Though he'd be willing to wager that wouldn't go down well with the clientele. He chuckled and scratched his chin, with its week's worth of grizzled whiskers. That crowd, mostly rough and ready fishermen, didn't have a high regard for the law, or for the cops who enforced it, either. No, close the Bilge before the customers were ready to call it a night, and there'd be a fine brouhaha.

And, anyway, he didn't sleep well these days, so there was no sense tossing out some poor soul before he was ready to go, because, truth be told, he didn't mind a bit of company in the wee hours. He knew that if he went home and to bed, he'd only be twisting and turning in the sheets, unable to calm his thoughts enough to sleep.

That's why he'd started tidying the bar at night instead of leaving it for the morning. The rhythmic tasks soothed him. Rinsing and drying the glasses, rubbing down the bar.

Wiping the tables, giving the floor a bit of a sweep. That's what he was doing, shuffling along behind a push broom to clear away all the dropped cigarette butts and matches and dirt carried in on cleated winter boots. He braced himself for the blast of cold and opened the door to sweep it all out, back where it belonged. But it wasn't the cold that took his breath away. It was a bird, a big crow, and it walked right in.

"And what do you think you're doing?" he demanded, feeling a large hollowness growing inside him.

"You know quite well, don't you?" replied the crow, hopping up onto the bar with a neat flap of his wings. The bird cocked his head and looked him in the eye. "Don't tell me an Irishman like you, born and bred in the old country, has forgotten the tale of Cú Chulainn?"

He'd not forgotten. He'd heard the story often as a boy, long ago in Ireland, where his mother dished up the old stories with his morning bowl of oats. "Eat up," she'd say, "so you'll be as strong as Cú Chulainn."

He found his mind wandering and followed it down the dark paths of memory. Had it really been that long? Sixty odd years? More than half a century? It seemed like yesterday that he was tagging along behind his ma when she made the monthly trek to the post office to pay the bills. " 'Tisn't the sort of thing you can forget," he told the crow. "Especially that statue in the Dublin General Post Office. A handsome piece of work that is, illustrating how Cú Chulainn knew death was near and tied himself to a post so he could die standing upright, like the hero he was."

"Cú Chulainn was a hero indeed," admitted the crow. "And his enemies couldn't kill him until the Morrighan lit on his shoulder, stealing his strength, weakening him. . . ."

"Right you are. The Morrighan," he said. The very thought of that fearsome warrior goddess, with her crimson cloak and chariot, set his heart to pounding in his bony old chest.

"And what form did the Morrighan take, might I ask?" inquired the bird.

"A crow," he said, feeling a great trembling overtake him. "So is that it? Are you the Morrighan come for me?"

"What do you think, Daniel Malone?" replied the crow, stretching out its wings with a snap and a flap and growing larger, until its great immensity blocked out the light— first the amber glow of the neon Guinness sign, then the yellow light from the spotted ceiling fixture, the greenish light from the streetlamp outside, and finally, even the silvery light from the moon—and all was darkness.

Chapter One

Maybe it was global warming, maybe it was simply a warmer winter than usual, but it seemed awfully early for the snow to be melting. It was only the last day of January, and in the little coastal town of Tinker's Cove, Maine, that usually meant at least two more months of ice and snow. Instead, the sidewalks and roads were clear, and the snow cover was definitely retreating, revealing the occasional clump of snowdrops and, in sheltered nooks with southern exposures, a few bright green spikes of daffodil leaves that were prematurely poking through the earth.

You could almost believe that spring was in the air, thought Lucy Stone, part-time reporter for the town's weekly newspaper, the *Pennysaver*. She wasn't sure how she felt about it. Part of her believed it was too good to be true, probably an indicator of future disasters, but right now the sun was shining and birds were chirping and it was a great day to be alive. So lovely, in fact, that she decided to walk the three or four blocks to the harbor, where she had an appointment to interview the new harbormaster, Harry Crawford.

As she walked down Main Street, she heard the steady drip of snow melting off the roofs. She felt a gentle breeze against her face, lifting the hair that escaped from her beret, and she unfastened the top button of her winter coat. Quite a few people were out and about, taking advantage of the unseasonably fine weather to run some errands, and everyone seemed eager to exchange greetings. "Nice day, innit?" and "Wonderful weather, just wonderful," they said, casting suspicious eyes at the sky. Only the letter carrier Wilf Lundgren, who she met at the corner of Sea Street, voiced what everyone was thinking. "Too good to be true," he said, with a knowing nod. "Can't last."

Well, it probably wouldn't, thought Lucy. Nothing did. But that didn't mean she couldn't enjoy it in the meantime. Her steps speeded up as she negotiated the hill leading down to the harbor, where the ice pack was beginning to break up. All the boats had been pulled from the water months ago and now rested on racks in the parking lot, shrouded with tarps or shiny white plastic shrink-wrap. The gulls were gone—they didn't hang around where there was no food—but a couple of crows were flying in circles above her head, cawing at each other.

"The quintessential New England sound," someone had called it, she remembered, but she couldn't remember who. It was true, though. There was something about their raspy cries that seemed to capture all the harsh, unyielding nature of the landscape. And the people who lived here, she thought, with a wry smile.

Harry Crawford, the new harbormaster, was an exception. He wasn't old and crusty like so many of the locals; he was young and brimming with enthusiasm for his job. He greeted Lucy warmly, holding open the door to his waterfront office, which was about the same size as a highway tollbooth. It was toasty inside, thanks to the sun streaming through the windows, which gave him a 360-degree view of the harbor and parking lot. Today he hadn't even switched on the small electric heater.

"Hi, Lucy. Make yourself comfortable," he said, pulling out the only chair for her to sit on. He leaned against the half wall, arms folded across his chest, staring out at the water. It was something people here did, she thought. They followed the water like a sunflower follows the sun, keeping a watchful eye out for signs that the placid, sleeping giant that lay on the doorstep might be waking and brewing up a storm.

"Thanks, Harry," she said, sitting down and pulling off her gloves. She dug around in her bag and fished out a notebook and pen. "So tell me about the Waterways Committee's plans for the harbor."

"Here, here," he said, leaning over her shoulder to unroll the plan and spread it out on the desk. "They're going to add thirty more slips, and at over three thousand dollars a season, it adds up to nearly a hundred thousand dollars for the town."

"If you can rent them," said Lucy.

"Oh, we can. We've got a waiting list." He shaded his eyes with his hand and looked past her, out toward the water. "And that's another good thing. A lot of folks have been on that list for years, and there's been a lot of bad feeling about it. You know, people are not really using their slips, but hanging on to them for their kids, stuff like that. But now we ought to be able to satisfy everyone."

Lucy nodded. She knew there was a lot of resentment toward those who had slips from those who didn't. It was a nuisance to have to ferry yourself and your stuff and your crew out to a mooring in a dinghy. With a slip, you could just walk along the dock to the boat, untie it, and sail off. "So you think this will make everybody happy?" she asked. "What about environmental issues? I understand there will be some dredging."

He didn't answer. His gaze was riveted on something outside that had caught his attention. "Sorry, Lucy. There's something I gotta check on," he said, taking his jacket off a hook.

Lucy turned and looked outside, where a flock of gulls and crows had congregated at the end of the pier. "What's going on?" she asked.

"The ice is breaking up. Something's probably come to the surface."

From the excited cries of the gulls, who were now arriving from all directions, she knew it must be something they considered a meal. A feast, in fact.

"Like a pilot whale?"

"Could be. Maybe a sea turtle, a dolphin even. Could be anything."

"I'd better come," she said, with a groan, reluctantly pulling a camera out of her bag.

"I wouldn't if I were you," he said, shaking his head. "Whatever it is, it's not going to be pretty, not this time of year. It could've been dead for months."

"Oh, I'm used to it," sighed Lucy, who had tasted plenty of bile photographing everything from slimy, half-rotted giant squid tentacles caught in fishing nets to bloated whale carcasses that washed up on the beach.

"Trust me. The stench alone . . ."

She was already beginning to feel queasy. "You've convinced me," she said, guiltily replacing her camera. Any photo she took would probably be too disgusting to print, she rationalized, and she could call him later in the day and find out what it was. Meanwhile, her interest had been caught by a handful of people gathered outside the Bilge, on the landward side of the parking lot. Tucked in the basement beneath a block of stores that fronted Main Street, the Bilge was a Tinker's Cove landmark—and a steady source of news. It was the very opposite of Hemingway's "clean, well-lighted place," but that didn't bother the fishermen who packed the place. It may have been a dark and dingy dive, but the beer was cheap, and Old Dan never turned a paying customer away, not even if he was straight off the boat and stank of lobster bait.

Lucy checked her watch as she crossed the parking lot and discovered it was only a little past ten o'clock. *Kind of early to start drinking,* she thought, but the three men standing in front of the Bilge apparently thought otherwise.

"It's never been closed like this before," said one. He was about fifty, stout, with white hair combed straight back from a ruddy face.

"Old Dan's like clockwork. You could set your watch by it. The Bilge opens at ten o'clock. No earlier. No later," said another, a thin man with wire-rimmed glasses.

"He closed once for a couple of weeks, maybe five or six years ago," said the third, a young guy with long hair caught in a ponytail, who Lucy knew played guitar with a local rock band, the Claws. "He went to Florida that time, for a visit. But he left a sign."

"What's up? Is the Bilge closed?" she asked.

They all turned and stared at her. Women usually avoided the Bilge, where they weren't exactly welcome. A lot of fishermen still clung to the old-fashioned notion that women were bad luck on a boat—and in general.

"I'm Lucy Stone, from the *Pennysaver,*" she said. "If the Bilge has really closed, that's big news."

"It's been shut tight for three days now," said the guy with the ponytail.

"Do you mind telling me your name?" she asked, opening her notebook. "It's Dave, right? You're with the Claws?"

"Dave Reilly," he said, giving her a dazzling, dimpled smile.

Ah, to be on the fair side of thirty once more, she thought, admiring Dave's fair hair, bronzed skin, full lips, and white teeth. *He must be quite a hit with the girls,* she decided, reminding herself that she had a job to do. "Has anybody seen Old Dan around town?" she asked.

"Come to think of it, no," said the guy with glasses.

"And your name is?" she replied.

"Brian Donahue."

"Do you think something happened to him?" she asked the stout guy, who was cupping his hands around his eyes and trying to see through the small window set in the door.

"Whaddya see, Frank?" inquired Dave. He turned to Lucy. "That's Frank Cahill. You'd never know it, but he plays the organ at the church."

"Is he inside? Did he have a heart attack or something?" asked Brian.

Frank shook his head. "Can't see nothing wrong. It looks the same as always."

"Same as always, except we're not inside," said Brian.

"Hey, maybe we're in some sort of alternate universe. You know what I mean. We're really in the Bilge in the real world, having our morning pick-me-up just like usual, but we're also in this parallel world, where we're in the parking lot," said Dave.

The other two looked at each other. "You better stick to beer, boy," said Frank, with a shake of his head. "Them drugs do a job on your brain."

"What am I supposed to do?" replied the rocker. "It's not my fault if Old Dan is closed, is it? A guy's gotta have something. Know what I mean?"

"You could try staying sober," said Lucy.

All three looked at her as if she were crazy.

"Or find another bar," she added.

"The others don't open 'til noon," said Brian. "Town bylaw."

"Old Dan has a special dispensation?" she asked.

The others laughed. "You could say that," said Dave, with a bit of an edge in his voice. "He sure doesn't play by the same rules as the rest of us."

"Special permission. That's good," said Brian.

"Yeah, like from the pope," said Frank, slapping his thigh. "I'll have to tell that one to Father Ed." He checked his watch. "Come to think of it, I wonder where he is? He usually stops in around now."

My goodness, thought Lucy, echoing her great-grandmother who had been a staunch member of the Woman's Christian Temperance Union. She knew there was a lot of drinking in Tinker's Cove, especially in the winter, when the boats sat idle. Some joker had even printed up bumper stickers proclaiming: "Tinker's Cove: A quaint little drinking village with a fishing problem," when government regulators had started placing tight restrictions on what kind of fish and how much of it they could catch and when they could catch it. She'd laughed when she first saw the sticker on a battered old pickup truck. After all, she wasn't above pouring herself a glass of wine to sip while she cooked supper. She certainly wasn't a teetotaler, but her Puritan soul certainly didn't approve of drinking in the morning.

The laughter stopped, however, when they heard a siren blast, and the birds at the end of the pier rose in a cloud, then settled back down.

"Something washed up," said Lucy, by way of explanation. "Probably a pilot whale."

The others nodded, listening as the siren grew louder and a police car sped into the parking lot, screeching to a halt at the end of the pier. The birds rose again, and this time they flapped off, settling on the roof of the fish-packing shed.

"I've got a bad feeling about this," said Dave. "Real bad."

He took off, running across the parking lot, followed by Brian and Frank. Lucy stood for a minute, watching them and considering the facts. First, Old Dan was missing, and second, a carcass had turned up in the harbor. She hurried after them but was stopped with the others at the dock by Harry, who wasn't allowing anyone to pass. At the end of the pier, she could see her friend Officer Barney Culpepper peering down into the icy water.

"I know Barney," she told Harry as she pulled her camera out of her bag. "He won't mind."

"He said I shouldn't let anybody by," insisted Harry, tilting his head in Barney's direction.

Lucy raised the camera and looked through the view-finder, snapping a photo of Barney staring down into the water. From the official way he was standing, she knew this was no marine creature that had washed up. "I guess it's not a pilot whale?" she asked, checking the image in the little screen.

Harry shook his head.

"It's a person, right?" said Dave. "It's Old Dan, isn't it?"

Lucy's fingers tightened on the camera. There was a big difference between jumping to a conclusion and learning it was true, a big difference between an unidentified body and one with a name you knew.

"I'm not supposed to say," said Harry.

"You don't have to," said Brian. "It's pretty obvious. The Bilge has been closed for days, and there's been no sign of him. He must've fallen in or something."

"Took a long walk off a short pier," said Dave, with a wry grin. "Can't say I'm surprised."

"He was known to enjoy a tipple," said Frank. He eyed the Bilge. "He'll be missed."

"What a horrible way to go," said Lucy, shivering and fingering her camera. "In the cold and dark and all alone."

"Maybe he wasn't alone," said Dave, raising an eyebrow.

"What do you mean?" asked Lucy. "Do you think some-body pushed him in?"

"Might have," said Frank. "He made a few enemies in his time."

Dave nodded. "You had to watch him. He wasn't above taking advantage, especially if you'd had a few and weren't thinking too hard."

Something in his tone made Lucy wonder if he was speaking from personal experience.

"And he wasn't exactly quick to pay his bills," said Brian, sounding resentful.

Another siren could be heard in the distance.

"So I guess he won't be missed," said Lucy.

"No, I won't miss the old bastard," said Frank. "But I'm sure gonna miss the Bilge."

The others nodded in agreement as a state police cruiser peeled into the parking lot, followed by the white medical examiner's van.

"The place didn't look like much," said Brian.

"But the beer was the cheapest around," said Dave.

"Where else could you get a beer for a buck twenty-five?" asked Frank.

The three shook their heads mournfully, united in grief.

Chapter Two

They stood in a little group, watching as a state trooper exited his cruiser and settled his cap on his head. "Step back, step back, and clear the way," he ordered, striding down the dock. Two white-suited technicians from the medical examiner's office followed in his wake, wheeling a stainless steel gurney fitted with a black body bag.

"C'mon, Harry," coaxed Frank. "Tell us what happened."

Harry swallowed hard and stared into the distance.

"It was bad, huh?" asked Brian.

Harry swallowed again, then made a dash for a trash barrel, where he leaned in and vomited.

"I guess it's bad," said Dave.

"Now, move on along," said Officer Barney Culpepper, who had left his post at the end of the dock to make room for the technicians to recover the body. "There's nothing to be seen here." He nodded toward Harry, who was still hanging on to the side of the trash barrel. "Nothing you want to see, believe me."

Nobody moved.

"Don't you folks have something better to do?" demanded Barney, jowls quivering. He looked a bit like a bulldog, with a pug nose and square face. Somehow the bulky blue cold-weather uniform, and his growing girth, only added to the impression.

"C'mon, Barney," said Lucy. "Can't you give me something for the paper? A body in the water is big news."

"Now, Lucy, you know I'm not supposed to make statements to the press. That's up to the captain."

"You don't have to make a statement," she said, pleading. "I won't even mention your name. I'll say a passerby discovered . . . what? What's in the water?"

Avoiding the others, Barney took her by the elbow and walked with her toward his cruiser. The three men followed at a distance, straining to hear, until he turned and snapped at them. "Can't you mind your own business!" Then, lowering his voice so only she could hear, he said, "It's Old Dan. At least I think it is. It's hard to tell."

"The body's decomposed?" she asked.

"You could say that."

"His face is gone?" Lucy knew that was common when a body had been in the water. Crabs and fish usually started with the bare skin of the face and hands.

"More than his face," said Barney.

Lucy noticed his usually ruddy face had gone white. Even Barney, a twenty-year veteran of the force, was shocked.

"More than his face?" she repeated.

"His whole head's gone."

Lucy didn't quite take it in. "The body's headless?"

Barney nodded.

Lucy considered this for a minute, thinking of the various bodies that were occasionally recovered from the sea around Tinker's Cove. Not one had been headless.

"Isn't that unusual?" she asked.

"It happens," he admitted. "The head's kinda heavy, and the connection isn't that strong, really, so if the body rolls around, it can sorta detach. Especially if it's helped along by the critters." He paused and scratched his chin. "But it usually takes longer. The rest of him seems pretty fresh, so I don't think he was in there more than a few days. And the cold shoulda preserved him. You know what I mean?"

Lucy nodded. "So all I can say is, an unidentified headless body was found and is presumed to be that of Old Dan, who has been missing for several days?"

"That sounds about right," he said, straightening his cap, "but you didn't hear it from me."

Lucy watched as he opened the car door and awkwardly squeezed behind the steering wheel, reaching for his radio. Then she turned and passed on her report to the three men. It only seemed fair. The sooner they got confirmation that Old Dan would definitely not be opening the Bilge, the sooner they could make other plans for their morning. But she kept one fact, the fact that the corpse was headless, to herself. That was a scoop if she ever saw one.

Eager to get back to the office and file her story, Lucy chugged up the hill and swung around the corner onto Main Street, where she collided with Father Ed O'Neil, the priest from Our Lady of Hope Church, nearly knocking him over. Father Ed was well into his sixties and had never been a large man. He was only an inch or two taller than Lucy and probably weighed less.

"Oh, Father Ed, I am so sorry," she apologized.

"No matter, no matter," said Father Ed, straightening his jacket and smoothing his red hair, which was liberally salted with white. "I should have looked where I was going."

"The fault was mine," said Lucy, wondering why the mere sight of his backwards collar seemed to inspire her to confess when she wasn't even Catholic. "Are you all right?"

"Fine, fine. Couldn't be finer," he said, bouncing on the balls of his feet and rubbing his hands together. "And why, may I ask, are you in such a hurry?"

"My deadline's at noon," said Lucy, pointing to her watch

and sidling past him. He was notoriously long-winded, and she didn't want to get trapped in a lengthy conversation.

He turned right along with her, maintaining eye contact and making it impossible for her to continue on her way without being rude. "And you have a big story?" He cocked his head.

"Not really," she said, with a shrug, guarding her scoop. She didn't want the news to get all over town before the paper hit the newsstands later this afternoon.

"Perhaps I can be of service," he suggested, planting himself firmly in her path. "I have some big news."

She was stuck, she realized. Father Ed wasn't going to let her go until she'd heard him out.

"Terrific," she said, hoping she didn't sound sarcastic. "Fire away, Father. We're always interested in the doings at Our Lady of Hope."

"Well," he said, "it's a bit of a story. Maybe we should find a place to sit down. I could buy you a cup of coffee at Jake's?"

"Oh, no, Father. As I said, I've got to get back. Deadline's at noon and . . ."

"All right," he said. "I'll be as brief as I can be. Did you know that this year is the one hundredth anniversary of Our Lady of Hope here in Tinker's Cove?"

"No, no, I didn't," said Lucy, looking with longing at the *Pennysaver* office, just across the street.

"Well, to be precise, it's just the anniversary of the building. The congregation is much older, started by émigrés from the famine, the Irish famine back in the 1840s. That was a terrible time, you know. So much suffering."

Lucy nodded. She knew about the terrible famine that had prompted so many Irish families to leave their homeland. "And you're doing something special to celebrate the anniversary?" she asked, prompting him.

"Yes, indeed. That we are."

"And what are you doing?" She prompted him again, conscious of the minutes ticking away.

"We are staging a gala show," he said, his blue eyes sparkling with excitement. "As you no doubt know, the church puts on a show every spring around St. Patrick's Day. Last year it was *Bye Bye Birdie,* and it was a terrific success."

"Yes, it was," agreed Lucy, who had gone with her husband, Bill, and her two youngest children, Sara and Zoe.

"So you saw it?"

"Yes, it was great. But what are you doing this year?"

"This year we're doing something special. Not that *Bye Bye Birdie* wasn't great. Why even you said it was. But for the hundredth anniversary, we really want something . . . What's the phrase? Something boffo." He clearly enjoyed rolling the words off his tongue. "We really want to *wow* everybody!"

"I'm sure you will," said Lucy, desperate to be on her way. "But what is the show?"

"Oh, I have it all right here," he said, pulling a folded piece of paper out of his jacket pocket.

It was only with the greatest difficulty that Lucy managed to restrain herself from grabbing the paper and running across the street to the office. Instead, she stood, tapping her foot, while he carefully unfolded it with his gloved hands.

"As you can see here," he said, pointing, "we're going to stage *Finian's Rainbow.* Now is this right? Is it clear enough? Mrs. Kelly always worries about getting her press releases done properly. In the correct format, if you know what I mean."

"It's fine. I'm sure it's fine," said Lucy.

"Now, whatever you do, don't miss this bit," he said, pointing to the second paragraph. "Because this is where we announce that the show is going to be directed by a professional actor. We may be amateurs, but we want this show to be as close to professional as we can make it. So we've hired this chap from Ireland who has considerable stage experience."

"Well, that's very wise," said Lucy. "I'll be sure to get every word in. Now if you'll just give me the press release . . ."

Father Ed was reading the paper, checking it one last time. "I think it's quite clear. It seems so to me. But if you have any questions . . ."

"I know where to reach you," said Lucy, snatching the paper.

"I'm at the church, you know," he called as she ran across the street.

"I know," she yelled back from the other side. Two more steps and she was across the sidewalk and yanking open the door, setting the little bell jingling.

"Where have you been?" bellowed Ted Stillings, the publisher, editor, and chief reporter. He was in his usual position, hunched over the computer that sat on the roll-top desk he'd inherited from his grandfather, an editor of some renown. Now pushing fifty, he still looked boyish, thanks to a full head of hair and an efficient metabolism. "Do you know the time? It's a quarter to twelve! It's a deadline, not a guideline, or have you forgotten?"

"Hold the presses," Lucy yelled back, thrilled to be able to utter the famous phrase. "I've got big news."

"This better be good," warned Phyllis, who multitasked as receptionist, listings editor, and classified ad manager. She raised her thinly plucked eyebrows over her colorful harlequin reading glasses. "He's in a state."

"This is big," said Lucy, savoring the moment. "Dan Malone's headless body was found floating in the harbor this morning."

Her announcement didn't have quite the effect she'd expected. Instead of stunned amazement, Phyllis expressed puzzlement. "Who's Dan Malone?" she asked. For his part, Ted was skeptical. "Are you sure?" he asked.

"Dan Malone is the proprietor of the Bilge, and he's been missing for three days," said Lucy.

"Filthy place," said Phyllis, dismissing the news with a shrug and returning to her listings.

Lucy continued. "And while I don't have an official identification, the fact remains that a dead body has been found in the icy water, and Old Dan has gone missing, and the bar's been closed for three days."

"Did you say this body is headless?" inquired Ted.

"Yes," said Lucy, exhaling vehemently.

"Probably happens all the time," said Phyllis. "Tides and whatnot."

"Not in three days," said Lucy, through clenched teeth. "At least that's what my expert source says."

"Who is your source?" asked Ted.

"Can't tell," said Lucy. "I promised."

"Barney Culpepper," said Phyllis. "Bet you a dollar."

"Not necessarily," said Lucy, sliding Father Ed's press release across the counter to Phyllis. "Last-minute listing. I promised you'd get it in."

Phyllis glared at her. She'd recently lost quite a bit of weight, and the new, skinny Phyllis wasn't nearly as agreeable as the jolly, plump one. Even her wardrobe had become more sedate, as she'd given up the brightly colored muumuus she favored when she was heavy for a more subdued professional look. "The listings deadline was noon yesterday," she said, adjusting the red and black scarf she'd tied over her gray turtleneck sweater.

"Oh, please. I promised Father Ed," begged Lucy.

"Why don't you type it yourself, then," said Phyllis, sliding it right back to her.

"Oh, all right." Lucy snatched it up. "And, Ted, do you want me to write up the body? I've got a photo."

"Of the body?" he asked eagerly.

"No. Of Barney Culpepper at the end of the pier, looking at it."

"See!" crowed Phyllis. "Didn't I say Barney was her secret source?"

"Sure," he said, with a sigh. "Keep it short and sweet. Just the facts. I'll download the photo."

"Okay," said Lucy. She plunked herself down at her desk, coat and all, and began typing.

"Just the facts," he repeated, taking her camera. "You've got twelve minutes."

She didn't need twelve minutes, however, considering the meager facts at her disposal. The most she could produce was a three-inch brief outlining the bare facts of the discovery of a headless body. She couldn't even get the police chief to give her a statement; his only comment was, "No comment."

That done, she shrugged off her winter coat and started in on Father Ed's press release, typing it practically verbatim, but stripping out the numerous laudatory adjectives. When she came to the "brilliant Dylan Malone," who would be directing the show, however, it seemed to be an accurate description. She deleted "brilliant," of course, but she couldn't help being impressed by a long string of credits, which included everything from classic roles at Dublin's Abbey Theatre to a part as a cop on a long-running BBC action adventure show. It all held up when she checked him out on Google, where there was even a photo of his handsome face, complete with a roguish smile.

She was studying the face and trying to guess his age when Ted broke into her reverie. "Are you done yet? It's past noon."

"Oh, right," she said, pulling herself away and typing in the final sentence. She hit SEND, shipping the file to Ted for final editing and leaned back in the chair, dramatically wiping her brow.

"Enough drama," snapped Phyllis. "You're just sitting and typing. It's not as if you're actually working."

"You know what I think? I think you need some chocolate," said Lucy. "I know I could sure use some. It's not every day that a headless body turns up and I have to cover it."

"Well, if it is Old Dan, it's no more than he deserved, if you ask me," said Phyllis, pursing her lips. "That Bilge place attracts a rough crowd. There's always fights and goodness knows what all."

"There's no arguing with that," said Lucy. "The police could have closed the place plenty of times, but they never did. Do you know why, Ted?"

Ted was in the middle of shipping the completed issue to the printer, via the Internet. When he finished, he stretched and leaned back in his chair. "Good job, ladies. Thanks for your hard work." Then he swiveled his chair around and leaned forward, placing his elbows on his knees. "You know what I think? I think it was one of those 'the devil you know is better than the one you don't' situations. They kept an eye on the place. They never let things get too out of hand. They kind of tolerated it as an escape valve for the town's rowdy element."

"Well, I never," exclaimed Phyllis. "Since when is it up to the police to decide which laws they're going to enforce?"

"I guess there's always a little bit of that. Not everything is black and white," replied Ted. "Cops have to make judgment calls all the time. Should they give a citation or a warning, for example, to the distracted mother with three kids in the car who goes through a stop sign?"

"A warning," said Lucy.

"A citation," said Phyllis.

Ted threw up his hands just as the door opened and a handsome man walked in, sporting a thick head of dark hair, an intricately knitted Irish fisherman's sweater, with a white silk scarf knotted around his neck, and a roguish grin. Lucy recognized him immediately, and her identification was confirmed when he stuck out his hand to Phyllis and, taking hers, lifted it to his lips, announcing himself in a thickly accented voice as "Dylan Malone, straight off the plane from Shannon Airport in Ireland."

"Enough of your nonsense," said Phyllis, snatching her hand back and blushing furiously, right up to the roots of her dyed orange hair. It was the one thing she hadn't changed.

"Look," exclaimed Lucy, jumping to her feet. "Your photo is still on my computer. I just wrote up the press release about *Finian's Rainbow*."

"Pleased to make your acquaintance," he said, taking her hand and leaning over it. "And you are?"

"Oh, how silly of me," dithered Lucy, uncomfortably aware that she, too, was blushing. "I'm Lucy Stone. I work here."

"So I see," he said. "And I'm sure you do a wonderful job."

"Don't be too sure," said Ted, getting to his feet and holding out his hand. "I'm Ted Stillings."

"He's the boss," said Phyllis, beaming at Dylan.

"Well, this is certainly a fine establishment, and Tinker's Cove is as fine a town as I've seen anywhere, even in my own country of Ireland," replied Dylan. "In fact, it's a bit like Ireland, with the sea and the rocky coast."

"I've never been to Ireland," said Lucy, "but I'd love to go."

"Oh, you should. You shouldn't miss it," said Dylan as he looked at her closely. "If I'm not mistaken, you've got a bit of Irish blood, haven't you?"

"Not that I know of," said Lucy. "A bit of everything but, I think."

"Oh, well, 'tis no matter. People are the same the world

over." He paused. "Now if I may, I wonder if you could help me?"

"Certainly," said Phyllis, succumbing to his charm. "What can we do for you?"

"Well, you see, we arrived this morning, myself and my wife, Moira, and our little girl, Deirdre, and the plan was that my brother would meet us at Logan Airport in Boston and bring us along here to Tinker's Cove. But he never turned up at the airport, and when I called him at his home here in Tinker's Cove, there was no answer, and there was no answer at his place of business, either. So we rented a car and came along, but I confess I'm a mite worried about him, and I wonder if you might know of his whereabouts."

It was suddenly very quiet in the newspaper office. Finally, after a long pause, Ted asked the question they all feared they knew the answer to. "What is your brother's name?"

"Why he's quite well known hereabouts, I believe. He's a publican and proprietor of a fine establishment known as the Bilge. He's Daniel Malone, that's who he is."

Chapter Three

The only sound in the *Pennysaver* office was the familiar click as the furnace switched on, followed a moment or two later by the whir of the fan that blew the heated air out through the register, making the venetian blinds rattle.

Dylan looked from one anxious face to another, reading the bad news in their expressions. "Something has happened to my brother?" he asked, raising his thick eyebrows.

"I'm afraid so," said Ted, clearing his throat. "It seems he went missing about three days ago."

"Missing? What do you mean?" said Dylan.

"The Bilge has been closed for three days," said Ted. "And there was no sign of Old Dan"—he paused and swallowed hard—"until this morning. They found a body in the harbor, and they think it's his."

Dylan seemed to sway on his feet, so Phyllis quickly wheeled her chair around from behind the counter and held it for him until he was safely seated. "Can I get you a glass of water?" she asked.

"A cup of tea?" suggested Lucy.

"I'm sorry to have to give you such terrible news," said Ted.

"Jesus, Mary, and Joseph," said Dylan, whose face had

gone quite white. "This is terrible news. Terrible news indeed," he said, shaking his head.

"I'm so sorry," said Lucy. "This must be a dreadful shock."

"Indeed it is," said Dylan, shaking his head. "He was in the best of health. He said he was in fine fettle. Those were his very words. 'Couldn't be finer,' he said last time I spoke with him." He looked at Lucy. "You say they found him in the harbor?"

"Well, they found a body in the harbor," replied Lucy. "They're not absolutely sure it's his."

Dylan seized upon this bit of information eagerly. "You say they're not sure? There's a chance it could be someone else?"

Lucy shook her head apologetically. "I don't think there's really any doubt that it's your brother. It's a formality really."

"Well then, why not say so?" asked Dylan.

Lucy looked at the wall, which featured a calendar with a photo of a tall-steepled white church nestled in snow-covered hills. Picture-perfect New England. "It's the condition of the body that's the problem."

Dylan furrowed those magnificent eyebrows. "But it's only been three days, and it's been very cold, hasn't it?"

Lucy sighed and looked at Ted, hoping for some help.

He stepped forward. "There's no easy way to tell you," he said. "The body is headless."

Dylan seemed to suffer a delayed reaction when he heard the word. It almost seemed to Lucy that he had been expecting it. But then he quickly exclaimed, "Dear God!" and covered his face with his hands. He remained in the chair, with his head bowed, for what seemed like a long time. Then, slowly, he seemed to rally and got to his feet. "Life goes on," he said. "There are things I must do. My wife and daughter are outside in the car. They can't sit there all day. And there's the body. I must see to that."

"Of course," said Ted. "Why don't I take you to the police station?"

Dylan nodded in agreement, then hesitated. "The police station is no place for my daughter," he said.

"Of course not," agreed Lucy. "She must be exhausted from her long trip."

"My wife, too," said Dylan. "We were going to stay at my brother's place, but now . . ."

"There's a lovely inn here in town," suggested Lucy. "It's quaint and quiet. . . ."

"You'd get off-season rates," said Phyllis.

"That sounds perfect," said Dylan. "It will be a great relief to me to get them settled." He got to his feet slowly, as if it required extreme effort. "I'll meet you outside. We're parked right in front. But give me a moment. I need to explain to my wife what's happened."

Once he was gone, the three exhaled a collective sigh.

"Talk about bad timing," said Lucy, rolling her eyes.

"I hope I never have to go through something like that again," declared Ted. "Telling the poor man his brother is dead."

Phyllis shook her head and clucked her tongue. "Hardly the family reunion they were hoping for." She sighed. "Well, you two better get going. I'll stay here and hold the fort."

Lucy and Ted put on their coats and went out to the sidewalk, waiting just outside the door until Dylan waved them over.

He was standing next to a white compact rental car, with his arm around a slim woman who was wrapped in a long black cape that was fastened at the neck by an intricate silver clasp with elaborate twists and knots. A large hood covered her head, but locks of curly red hair escaped and were whipped by the wind against her lightly freckled cheeks. Her features were delicate, and she had large green eyes and a little, pointed chin.

"Meet my wife, Moira," said Dylan.

"Pleased to meet you," said Lucy, extending her hand. Moira took it with both gloved hands. "I'm Lucy Stone. I'll take you over to the inn while Ted, Ted Stillings, goes to the police station with your husband."

"Thank you so much," said Moira, speaking in a breathy little voice. "I really appreciate your help."

"We're glad to help," said Lucy. "Shall I drive?"

"That would be best," said Dylan. "Moira's not used to American cars yet."

Lucy opened the driver side door and saw a little girl, just about the same age as her own daughter Zoe, sitting in the backseat. "Hi, there," she said, sliding behind the steering wheel while Moira got settled in the passenger seat.

"Deirdre, me darling, what's happened to your manners? What do you say to Lucy here, who's going to take us to the hotel?"

The little girl sat a bit straighter and piped up. "How do you do?"

"Very well indeed, thank you," said Lucy. "And in just a few minutes, we'll have you settled nice and comfy at the Queen Victoria Inn."

The Queen Vic offered the best lodging in Tinker's Cove. It was built in the late nineteenth century, when the expansion of the railroads made it possible for city dwellers to escape the summer heat in the mountains or at the seashore. Large hotels were built to meet the demand for accommodations, and several had been built in Tinker's Cove, but only the Queen Vic had survived. It had been renovated, of course, and now boasted luxurious king-size beds and marble baths, but the roomy wrap-around porch, with its ranks of rocking chairs, and the dining room and parlors remained much the same as they had looked over a hundred years ago. Antique furniture stood on thick, plush rugs; crisp white curtains hung at the windows; and enormous potted plants filled the corners.

"This is quite charming," exclaimed Moira, cutting quite a dramatic figure as Lucy held the door for her and she swept up to the registration desk, with the cape streaming behind her. Once there she lifted the hood back with a graceful motion and shook her red hair loose.

"I'll go and get the bags," offered Lucy, who didn't want to intrude while Moira went through the business of getting a room. Then, stifling a stab of resentment when she found herself wrestling two oversized suitcases up the steps, she wondered why she'd been so quick to volunteer for bellhop duty. Once inside, she toted the wheeled bags down the hall, following Moira, who was holding the room key in one hand and Deirdre's little hand in the other.

Lucy felt rather awkward once they were inside the room, so she quickly took her leave. "I'm sure you want to get settled," she began, "but let me give you my phone number. . . ."

"Oh, Lucy, don't run off," said Moira, removing her cape and laying it on the bed. She then sat down and started unzipping Deirdre's little pink parka. As she watched the cozy domestic scene, Lucy could practically feel her heart melting and oozing with sympathy. She could only imagine what it must be like to be alone and adrift in a strange country.

With her coat removed, Deirdre was revealed to have her father's dark hair and her mother's little, pointed chin, along with a pair of the biggest, greenest eyes and the longest lashes Lucy had ever seen. Moira sent her into the bathroom to wash her hands, and when she emerged, she stood in the doorway and gave an enormous yawn.

"I think perhaps it's time for a nap," said Moira, settling the little girl on a chaise lounge that sat in the corner, covering her with her cape. "Mommy will be right down the hall," she said, smoothing the child's hair and giving her a kiss. "Come along, Lucy. Let's see if they can give us a cup of tea while we get acquainted."

Once again, Lucy found herself following Moira, who was wearing a long black skirt and an emerald green cashmere sweater, down the hall to the parlor, where they perched on an extremely curvy and lavishly carved Victorian sofa. Moira seemed to do little more than snap her fingers and a tea tray magically appeared, complete with finger sandwiches and an assortment of little cakes and cookies.

"You must be famished," said Lucy, helping herself to a cream cheese and date-nut bread sandwich. She certainly was, since she hadn't had lunch yet.

"No, not really," said Moira, lifting the teapot and pouring. "I always feel bloated after a transatlantic flight. They give you too much food, and you can't move around much."

This was news to Lucy. She hadn't heard anybody complain of too much food on an airplane flight for some time now.

"In the States, it's a tiny bag of five peanuts and a little cup of soda—if you're lucky," she said, but Moira ignored her conversational gambit.

"Can you tell me what really happened to Dan?" she asked, placing one hand on Lucy's knee and leaning toward her. "I didn't want to talk about it in front of Deirdre, you see."

"Of course," said Lucy, unconsciously recrossing her legs so Moira had to move her hand. "All I know is that they found a body in the harbor, and they think it's Old Dan. That's what everybody called him here," she added, by way of apology. "Did you know him well?"

"Never met him," said Moira, taking a sip of milky tea. "He moved to America years before Dylan and I got married."

"Was Dylan close to his brother?"

"Not really," she said, replacing her cup in its saucer. "I was a bit surprised when Dylan said he wanted to take this directing job because it would give him a chance to get reacquainted with his brother. It's a bit of a busman's holiday, really. Combining work with a family reunion." She gave a little tinkly laugh. "A very small family reunion to be sure, since there are only the four of us." Her hand fluttered to her mouth. "Ah, me, now it's only three."

"I know Dylan is supposed to direct *Finian's Rainbow* at the church," said Lucy, helping herself to a second little triangle of chicken salad on white bread. "Do you think he'll still do it?"

Moira seemed shocked at the question. "Of course. The show must go on!"

"Not really," said Lucy. "I mean, I'm sure the church could find someone else if your husband finds it too difficult to carry on."

Moira shook her head emphatically, making her long, curly locks bounce. "He's a professional. It wouldn't cross his mind to quit." She took another sip of tea. "Besides, there will be business to attend to. Daniel had a pub, and a house, too? I believe he was doing quite well. At least that's what we were given to think back in Ireland."

"I don't really know," confessed Lucy. "The Bilge was popular, and he did a good business, but I don't know if he owned the building or not. As for the house, I don't have any idea of its value."

Moira tilted her head back and ran her fingers through her hair. "Tinker's Cove seems like quite a prosperous place. All the houses are well kept. Business seems to be thriving. I suppose property values have risen considerably over the last few years?"

Lucy was a bit taken aback. Was she already calculating her husband's likely inheritance? "Like everywhere, I guess," said Lucy. "There is still quite a bit of poverty here."

"Really? I wouldn't have thought so."

"A lot of traditional industries, like fishing, are disappearing, and people have a hard time finding jobs that pay well. And then there are immigrants. Brazilians, Haitians, Somalians, all sorts of people are turning up. There's plenty of work for them in the summer, what with the tourists and all, but it all disappears come winter. It's a real problem, and there doesn't seem to be an easy solution."

Moira's expression made it clear she really wasn't interested in other people's problems. "I really ought to check on Deirdre," she said, standing up.

"She's a lovely little girl," said Lucy. "I have a daughter about her age. Zoe's ten. Perhaps she'd like to come and play with her?"

"That's very kind of you," said Moira, with a little smile. "She's already saying that she misses her friends from home."

"We'd love to have her visit . . . anytime at all," said Lucy. "Here. Let me write my home number on my card. Most of the time you can reach me at the paper, though."

Moira took the card and studied it. "Do you have a mobile?" she asked, pen in hand.

Lucy recited the number, wondering exactly where the pen had materialized from. Was it in her pocket? Lying on a side table? Was it summoned out of thin air? It was beginning to seem like a very long and confusing day. She needed some time to herself to sort things out.

"I've got to go," said Lucy. "I hope you'll be comfortable here, and let me know if I can do anything for you."

"You're too kind," boomed a hearty voice behind her, and she turned to see Dylan coming through the door. He stopped in the middle of the room and looked around appreciatively. "And a fine place you've found for us." He took a deep breath and placed his hands on his wife's shoulders. "Ah, Moira me darling, you'll find people here are very kind and welcoming. We got off to a bit of a rough start, I'll admit, but things are going to be fine. You'll see."

"Of course, they are, Dylan," replied Moira, stroking his cheek. "So tell me. Were you able to identify the body? Is it really your brother, Dan?"

He bowed his head, resting his chin on his chest for a moment, then raised it and gazed at the ceiling, revealing a glistening tear in the corner of his eye. "I'm afraid there's no doubt," he said, shaking his head sadly. "His wallet and his driver's license were found in his pocket." He blinked furiously, attempting to hold back the tears that were threatening to come. "He had an Irish penny in his pocket."

"For luck," said Moira, pressing her sobbing husband's face to her breasts.

Lucy felt like a voyeur, but she couldn't take her eyes off the grieving couple.

"Not that it did him much good," mumbled Dylan.

"That's not for us to judge, Dylan," said Moira, pronouncing her words in an even thicker accent. "For all we know, he had some sort of terrible cancer and was spared a painful, lingering death. We don't know the whole story, do we? We only see a little bit, here and there, as if we're looking through a telescope."

Her words seemed to give Dylan strength, and he straightened up. "You're right. It's not for me to despair, but to press on. That's what Daniel would want, wouldn't he?"

"That's the Malone way," said Moira.

"Aye, the Malone way. And Daniel was every bit a Malone." He suddenly seemed inspired. "And we can't let him leave this world without giving him a proper farewell. We're going to give him a genuine old-style Irish wake, right there in the bar. That's what we're going to do." He made eye contact with Lucy. "And will you help us get the word out that the whole town is invited?"

Lucy readily agreed to run an announcement in the paper, but as she finally made her escape and hurried back to the office, she couldn't help wondering if the scene she'd just witnessed had been genuine or if it had been staged for her benefit. She wanted to believe them, but she couldn't help remembering that they were actors, after all, trained to manipulate the audience's emotions.

Chapter Four

Lucy always woke with a wonderful sense of freedom on Thursday mornings. The deadline had come and gone, and, for better or worse, the past week's work had been committed to paper and ink. This week's edition was on its way to the readers, stacked and ready for purchase at the Quik Mart and IGA, and perhaps, even now, arriving in subscribers' mailboxes.

Ted wouldn't be in the office until the eleven o'clock budget meeting, which meant Lucy would have most of the morning to herself, once she got her husband, Bill, a restoration carpenter, off to work and the two youngest girls, Zoe and Sara, off to school. The older children, Toby and Elizabeth, had pretty much flown the nest. Toby, the firstborn and only boy, and his fiancée, Molly, had bought a house together on nearby Prudence Path and were expecting their first child. Elizabeth, next in line, was a junior at Chamberlain College in Boston.

Lying in bed, savoring the final few moments before the alarm went off, Lucy found her mind turning to Toby and Molly. She didn't understand why they weren't married, weren't even thinking about it, even though the baby was due to arrive in only a few months. She was happy about the pregnancy and excited about the prospect of becoming a grandmother, but she would be a lot happier if the baby's parents were married. She had even raised the topic, tact-fully, with Toby, but to no avail. "It's just a ceremony, a piece of paper," Toby had insisted. "It doesn't mean any-thing. We feel married."

The alarm sounded, and Lucy gave a little humph as she reached to turn it off. "I don't care what Toby says. Feel-ing married isn't the same as being married," she told Bill as she sat up and reached for her slippers with her feet.

"It's too early in the morning to start that again," said Bill, yawning and stretching.

Lucy gave him a sharp look. "Sometimes I think you're on Toby's side. Don't you care that your grandchild is going to be illegitimate?"

"Not really," he said, with a shrug, as he stood up. "I don't think it matters all that much."

Lucy also got up, and they stood facing each other across the bed. "Of course, it matters. People should be married before they have children. That's just the way it is. Bringing a life into the world is a big responsibility. What kind of parents will they be if they can't even decide to get married?"

Bill sighed. "They're going to be fine parents. What matters to me is that the baby is healthy. That's what's im-portant."

"Babies need stability to thrive," said Lucy. "That's why marriage is important: to create a stable home."

"Marriage doesn't create a stable home," said Bill, padding across the floor to the door, where he turned. "You know that as well as I do. Sometimes I think the real reason you want Toby and Molly to get married is so you and the girls can plan a wedding."

Lucy smiled, thinking of the three women she was going to meet for breakfast: Sue, Pam, and Rachel. They had been friends ever since they were young mothers, a tight group who minded each other's kids, got together for potluck suppers, and shared tears and laughter. When the kids got older and they found themselves drifting apart, they started getting together for breakfast every Thursday to keep in touch. They eagerly followed reports on each other's children, and Lucy would have liked nothing better than to announce that Toby and Molly had finally set the date.

The buzz was louder than usual when Lucy arrived at Jake's Donut Shack. Old Dan's death was big news, especially to the crowd of unemployed fishermen and construction workers who began the day with a leisurely breakfast at Jake's, then drifted over to the Bilge, where they remained until it was time for dinner. Even if they didn't read the *Pennysaver*, and Lucy suspected most of that crowd was not subscribers, word had spread quickly about the gruesome find in the harbor. The story had even been picked up by the morning radio and TV news, but they didn't provide any more information than Lucy had in her three-inch brief.

The crowd at Jake's all knew each other, and conversation was often general, including the whole room. "You know what this reminds me of?" asked one gray-haired fellow seated at the counter, who Lucy knew was a retired lobsterman. "That old 'set her again' joke."

"What joke's that, Walt?" asked someone, giving him an opening to continue. Lucy stopped to listen, as did most everybody else.

"Well," began Walt, "there was this lobstahman who took his wife out in the boat with him one day to help set the traps. Now a woman doesn't belong in a lobstah boat, everybody knows that, but maybe he wasn't feeling good or something that day. Anyhow, as you'd expect, it wasn't long before she began to scold him, telling him he wasn't doing this or that right, and as it happened, whether by accident or on purpose I can't say, but it so happened that she fell right out of the boat and into the water."

The gang at the counter nodded and laughed knowingly.

"Well, this poor lobstahman was kinda sad and depressed about it all, 'cause even though she was a scold, she did keep him warm at night, and now all he had was the dog, a smelly old Labrador, with whiskahs longer than his wife's."

By now the crowd was having a great old time, nudging each other and slapping their knees.

"So, like I said, being kind of depressed, he went for a walk along the beach with an old buddy who helped him set lobstah traps now and again, and what to his amazement did he see, but his wife's body, washed up on the shore, with twelve or thirteen big lobsters hanging on her. As you know, it wasn't a pretty sight, and the lobstahman was very upset. 'What should I do?' he asked. 'Well,' said his buddy, 'if I was you, I'd set her again.' "

At this the room exploded in loud, raucous laughter. All except for Lucy's friends, who were seated at their usual table.

"I've lived here for more than twenty years," she said, joining them, "but I'll never appreciate Maine humor."

"It is a terrible joke," agreed Rachel Goodman, who was known for her soft heart. She often convinced her lawyer husband, Bob, to take hopeless cases pro bono.

"Especially considering that poor man they found in the harbor," agreed Pam Stillings, who was married to Lucy's boss, Ted.

"It could almost put you off eating lobster," chimed in Sue Finch, who prided herself on her gourmet cooking. "But not quite," she added, and they all laughed.

"So tell us, Lucy. What's the inside scoop on Old Dan?" asked Rachel, taking a sip of the healthful herb tea she'd taken to drinking instead of coffee. Jake's didn't serve it; she brought the tea bags from home and ordered a pot of hot water.

"No inside scoop this time. You know as much as I know," replied Lucy.

"Ted told me Old Dan's brother is in town, along with his wife and child," said Pam, checking that the dangling silver earrings she'd worn since college were still in place.

"For the funeral? That was fast," said Sue, who was checking her BlackBerry for messages. She was in the process of opening a new business, Little Prodigies Preschool, and it was never far from her mind.

"No, no. He's an actor," said Lucy. "He's going to direct the spring show at Our Lady of Hope."

"And she said she didn't have the inside scoop!" exclaimed Rachel.

"So what can I get you ladies this morning?" asked Norine, the waitress, setting a cup and saucer in front of Lucy and filling it with coffee. "The usual?" she asked, going round the table and topping off the others' cups. "Hash and eggs over easy for Lucy, egg white omelet and whole wheat toast for Rachel, French toast for Pam and"—she cocked a disapproving look at Sue—"black coffee for her."

"I ate at home," said Sue, who weighed herself every morning and restricted herself to water if she gained an ounce over what she considered to be her ideal weight, 110 pounds.

"Like hell," growled Norine, marching off to give Jake the order.

"What's it to her if I don't want to look like a blimp?" complained Sue.

"You really shouldn't skip breakfast," advised Rachel. "It's the most important meal of the day."

"That's absurd," countered Sue, taking a sip of coffee. "The most important meal is cocktails. . . ."

"And you never skip that!" finished Lucy.

"Darned tootin'," said Sue, grinning.

"So what's this Dylan like?" asked Pam. "Ted says he's very Irish, whatever that means."

"You could say that," said Lucy. "And he's very much the actor. He was wearing a white fisherman's sweater and a silk scarf. Very eye-catching."

"Interesting," said Sue, who was by far the best dressed of the group, in a clingy black turtleneck sweater and tailored wool slacks. Unlike most of the women in Tinker's Cove, she even wore heels. "What about the wife?"

"Also very dramatic," said Lucy. "She was wearing a cape, a long one with a hood, and she has gorgeous red hair. They have a little girl, too, and she's adorable."

"And he's going to direct the show? Is that what you said?" asked Rachel. "They came all this way for an unpaid, volunteer job?"

"No, he's getting paid. Father Ed told me they'd hired a professional," said Lucy. "The wife, that's Moira, said it's a busman's holiday. Combining a family visit with a job."

Hearing Rachel humming a scrap of a tune, Lucy glanced at her curiously.

Rachel blushed. "It's from the show they're putting on: *Finian's Rainbow.* I was in it in college. It was great fun."

"I didn't know you acted," said Pam.

"Isn't she the sly one!" said Sue.

"What part did you play?" asked Lucy, ever the reporter.

"I was Sharon. The lead," replied Rachel. "I sang and danced and fell in love with the leading man."

"In the play or in real life?" asked Lucy.

"Both," said Rachel

"I bet it wasn't Bob," teased Pam.

Rachel smiled. "It wasn't Bob."

They were prevented from pursuing this line of inquiry when Norine arrived with the plates of food, and they all dug in. Except Sue, of course, who continued to sip her coffee and fiddle with her BlackBerry.

Rachel put down her fork. "You know what would be fun? Let's all be in the show!"

"We're not members of the church," said Pam.

"It doesn't matter," insisted Rachel. "It said in the announcement that everybody is invited to audition." Noticing the lack of enthusiasm on the part of the others, she continued. "It will be fun! Honest. The songs are great, and the story is so funny. It would be a blast."

"I can't sing," said Lucy.

"I get stage fright," said Pam.

"I'm too busy," said Sue. "I mean it. I'm flat out with the preschool."

"Well, I admit Sue does have a lot going on right now," conceded Rachel. "But, Lucy and Pam, aren't you the ones who always say winter is unbearable because it goes on forever and there's nothing to do and spring never seems to come?"

Lucy had to admit the words had a familiar ring. "Okay," she said. "I'll try out, but they'll never pick me."

"I'll give it my best shot," said Pam, "but I can't guarantee I'll show up on opening night."

"Believe me," declared Rachel, "you won't want to miss it!"

Fueled by too much caffeine and a dollop of guilt over the huge, cholesterol-rich breakfast she'd consumed, Lucy hurried to the newspaper office to get a head start on the coming week. She hadn't had a chance to write up the story about the harbor project. There would certainly be new developments in Old Dan's death, and there were always listings, those press releases announcing ham and bean dinners, dance recitals, and new books at the library.

"Well, aren't you the early bird," said Phyllis when she sailed through the door a bit before ten o'clock.

Since this was later than her usual time, but earlier than she needed to be there, she wasn't sure if she was being congratulated or chided. It was hard to tell with Phyllis these days. "I thought I'd get a head start on the listings," she said, hoping to smooth Phyllis's perpetually ruffled feathers.

"I haven't got them sorted yet," sniffed Phyllis. It was her job to open the mail and file the press releases by date.

"I can do that. No problem," said Lucy, who knew Phyllis had been busy all week collecting information for the tax preparer.

Phyllis considered this. "Okay," she finally said, as if she were doing Lucy a favor instead of the other way around. "Oh, this came for you," she said, handing Lucy a pink "While You Were Out" slip.

"I haven't had one of these in ages," said Lucy, unfolding it.

"I guess they don't have voice mail in Ireland," sniffed Phyllis. "She insisted I take a message."

Indeed, the message was from Moira, asking Lucy to call her at the inn. Lucy sat down at her desk and dialed the number on the slip and was immediately connected to Moira's room.

"Thanks so much for calling," said Moira, speaking with that Irish accent, which almost made Lucy think she could smell the shamrocks. "I hate to bother you but . . ."

"It's no bother," said Lucy, wondering if shamrocks did actually have an odor.

"Well, there's so much to do for the wake and all, and none of it is very interesting to a child."

Probably like grass, thought Lucy, *or maybe clover.* "Of course not," she said. "Would she like to come and play with Zoe this afternoon? You could bring her over at three thirty or so, when the girls get home from school."

"You're a lifesaver, Lucy," said Moira when Lucy had finished giving her directions to the house.

"I'm happy to do it," said Lucy, basking in the warm glow of a good deed. "I'll see you then."

She spent the next half hour opening the mail and sorting it, keeping an eye out for possible leads for a feature story. *Maybe an interview with Dylan,* she thought, opening the fourth copy of the *Finian's Rainbow* audition announcement. Mrs. Kelly apparently believed that the more copies she sent, the greater the chances it would actually appear in the paper. Lucy was tossing the extras in the trash when Ted arrived, looking rested and refreshed, with his hair still wet from the shower. The good mood didn't last long; it usually evaporated as soon as he spied a typo in the paper.

Lucy held her breath as he plucked a paper off the stack on the reception counter and scanned the front page. He nodded happily, turning the pages all the way through the local news, the editorials, even the sports. The frown didn't appear until he got to the legal ads announcing upcoming hearings. "Hysterical Commission?" he bellowed. "Hysterical!!"

Phyllis wasn't about to be cowed. "Freudian slip," she said, peering over her glasses. "They turned down my cousin Elfrida's paint color."

"About time she painted that house," said Ted. "What color did she want?"

"Black and white."

"Those are approved colors," said Ted. "What's the problem?"

"She wanted zebra stripes."

Lucy was giggling at her desk, earning a warning stare from Ted. "So you decided to get back by playing a little joke on them, is that it?" he asked.

"Not at all," said Phyllis, continuing to punch numbers into the adding machine. "Anyone can make a mistake."

"I give up," said Ted, throwing his arms up. "Let's figure out the news budget for next week." He strode across the little office and sat down at his desk, swirling his chair around, flipping his notebook open, and propping one ankle on the other knee.

"I'll follow up on Old Dan," volunteered Lucy.

"I'm on it," said Ted, reaching for a pen and adding a check to the list in his notebook.

"That's not fair," protested Lucy. "I had it first."

"I've got something else for you," said Ted. "You know those guys with the metal detectors that you see poking around everywhere. I want you to write about them."

Lucy's jaw dropped. "You're stealing my story, and you want me to write about old guys with metal detectors?"

"Calm down, Lucy. It's a good story," said Ted. "They turn up lost jewelry, valuable coins, all sorts of stuff. You can make a really interesting, prizewinning story out of it. Give it that Lucy Stone treatment."

"Flattery will get you nowhere, Ted. You're too obvious."

Phyllis chimed in. "You can say that again."

Lucy glared at him. "So what's the real story here, Ted?"

He bowed his head. "You're right. Normally, I'd let you cover Old Dan since you broke the story, but this one isn't for you. It looks like it's going to get nasty."

Phyllis and Lucy were all ears. "What do you mean?" asked Lucy.

"Well, I stopped at the police station on the way here, and they just got the preliminary autopsy results, and the word is that Old Dan didn't lose his head from natural causes. It was sliced off with a blade of some sort."

Phyllis and Lucy looked at each other, then back at Ted.

"A freak accident?" suggested Phyllis.

"That doesn't sound like an accident to me," mused Lucy. "Somebody must have killed him."

Ted shrugged. "That's what it looks like. He was beheaded."

"That's disgusting," said Phyllis, adding a disapproving sniff.

All of a sudden, Lucy got it. Ted thought a beheading was an unsuitable subject for a woman. "So you're not let-

ting me cover it, because it's a beheading?" demanded
Lucy, furiously. "Like I never heard of Anne Boleyn? Or
Charles I? Or Marie Antoinette? Like I never read *A Tale
of Two Cities*? That's your reason? Because I'm a girl, is
that it?"

Ted shook his head. "No. Not because it's gruesome.
Lord knows, you love that stuff. Because it's dangerous,
that's why. Some crazy guy with a machete or hatchet or
something sharp is running around loose, and I don't want
you tangling with him, that's why."

Lucy wasn't impressed. "Oh, so it's for my own good, is
it? Like I can't take care of myself."

"Enough." Ted put up his hands. "I'm the boss, and it's
my decision. That's all there is to it. I'm covering Old Dan,
and you're writing about old guys with metal detectors."

"Okay, Ted," fumed Lucy, reaching for her coat. "We'll
see who wins the Pulitzer."

"That's the spirit," said Ted as Lucy pushed the door,
with its little jangling bell, open and marched outside. "If
anyone can do it," he told Phyllis, "she can."

"You'll be sorry," said Phyllis, reaching for the phone.
"Elfrida? That you?" She chuckled nastily. "Did you see
the paper this morning? The legal ads?"

Chapter Five

Lucy took Shore Road home, keeping an eye out for the metal detector prospectors she was supposed to write about, but didn't spot any. She had a feeling this story wasn't going to be as easy to get as Ted thought. That was so typical, she decided. He'd see something—like maybe a kid with a weird haircut or a mom with a baby in a new-fangled backpack or, in this case, some old guy with a metal detector—and decide it was a trend and absolutely had to be covered. And she was always the lucky one who got to track down these elusive trendsetters and extract a story from them.

She turned onto Red Top Road, behind the school bus, and braked when it stopped, first at the new development of houses on Prudence Path and again at her own drive-way, where she watched as Zoe and Sara got off and ran to the house. They were already in the kitchen, shedding their coats and book bags, when she arrived.

"Don't leave that stuff on the kitchen floor," she told them. "Zoe's got a playdate."

"Is Sadie coming?" asked Zoe, who at ten years of age was obediently hanging her coat on the hook. Sadie was her best friend and a frequent playmate.

Sara, age fourteen, was ignoring her mother and look-ing for a snack in the refrigerator. "How come we don't have any string cheese?" she asked. "All my friends' moms buy string cheese."

"Sounds disgusting," said Lucy. "Have some yogurt instead, after you pick that stuff up off the floor."

"I don't like yogurt," replied Sara.

"Have a glass of milk," said Lucy. "There are chocolate chip cookies in the cookie jar. . . ."

"Mom, she'll eat 'em all!" protested Zoe. "There won't be any for me and Sadie."

"Like I'd even eat your disgusting cookies," said Sara, scooping up her coat and backpack and stomping up the stairs. "Like I want to weigh five hundred pounds."

"Sadie's not coming," said Lucy, giving Zoe a hug. "It's somebody new. Her name is Deirdre. She's far from home, she lives in Ireland, and she needs a friend while she's here in Maine."

"Okay," said Zoe, agreeably. "When is she coming?"

If only they could stay ten forever, thought Lucy. "I think I hear a car now," she said.

They went over to the window and watched as the little white rental car rolled to a stop by the porch steps and the doors popped open. Once out of the car, however, Deirdre hung back shyly until her mother took her by the hand and led her up the porch steps to the kitchen door. Lucy greeted them with a smile.

"I really appreciate this, Lucy. You have no idea," said Moira, kneeling down to unzip Deirdre's pink parka and handing it to Lucy.

"It's no trouble at all," said Lucy, hanging it on one of the hooks by the door. The girls seemed to be hitting it off immediately, she noticed with relief, and were heading for the family room, hand in hand, to look at a book Deirdre had brought.

"I'm almost out of my mind. Things have been that crazy," said Moira, pushing her unruly mop of red hair back with her hands. "The police, the people from the funeral home, the priest . . . There's always something to do, somebody to call. And poor Dylan! This was the last thing he expected. He thought his brother would be taking care of us."

"It must be very upsetting," sympathized Lucy. "How is he coping?"

"About as well as can be expected," said Moira, and before Lucy could even offer her a cup of tea, she was at the door. "I'll be back at six or so," she said, departing in a swirl of black cape.

Lucy set up a snack tray with a plate of cookies and two glasses of milk and carried it into the family room, where the girls were kneeling at the coffee table, poring over Deirdre's book.

"What's the book about?" she asked.

"Fairies and little people," said Deirdre. "May I have a biscuit?"

"Of course," said Lucy, struck by her politeness. "They're for you and Zoe to share. Drink some milk, too."

"Thank you," said Deirdre, taking a bite of cookie and a swallow of milk. "These biscuits are very good."

"They're not biscuits. They're cookies," said Zoe.

"In Ireland we call them biscuits," replied Deirdre.

"Biscuits are something else here," said Lucy. "They're soft, like bread. I'll make some for you sometime. They're really good with butter and jam."

"I'd like that. Thank you very much," said Deirdre, turning the page. "Oh, look, Zoe! This is Meab, the queen of the fairies."

Pleased that the little girls were getting along so well, Lucy went back to the kitchen and started browning some beef-stew meat. As she peeled and chopped the carrots and onions and turned the meat, she kept an ear out for squabbles, but all she heard from the family room was an occasional giggle. The afternoon passed quickly, and Lucy was calling Sara to set the table—for the third time—when Moira returned.

"And how did the little colleens get along?" she asked.

"Wonderfully," said Lucy. "I've hardly heard a peep all afternoon. Deirdre's a delight. She's so polite."

"Never fear. She has her moments," said Moira.

"They all do," agreed Lucy, going into the family room to fetch the little girl. "Your mom's here. It's time to go home."

"Already!" wailed Zoe.

"Oh, please, can't I stay a bit longer?" asked Deirdre.

"Yeah. Can't she stay longer?" chimed in Zoe.

"I'm afraid not," said Moira, who had followed Lucy. She glanced around the room, and Lucy wished she'd done something about the stains in the carpet and the worn place on Bill's recliner. But Moira didn't seem to notice. "What a lovely room," she declared. "I love rooms that have that lived-in look." She turned back to Deirdre. "It's time to go now, Deirdre. Your father's expecting us."

"But can't I play just a wee bit longer?" asked Deirdre.

What with those lashes and that adorable accent, Lucy thought the child was good enough to eat. But her mother wasn't moved. Her voice was firm when she said, "That's enough now. It's time to go."

"Perhaps you can come another day," suggested Lucy. "Maybe even sleep over."

"Wouldn't that be fun," said Moira, taking Deirdre's hand and leading her to the kitchen, where she helped her into her parka. "But now it's time to say good-bye and come away. Just like in the poem by Mr. Yeats. 'Come away, O human child! / To the waters and the wild / With a faery, hand in hand,' " she recited, dropping her voice theatrically, " 'For the world's more full of weeping than you can understand.' "

A funny poem to recite to a child, thought Lucy as she waved good-bye from the door. She thought her job as a parent meant protecting her children from the world's weeping, but maybe that was an American idea. Come to think of it, most of the old fairy stories were full of frightening ideas. She had hardly turned away from the door and returned to the stove to check her stew when Bill came breezing in.

"Something smells delicious," he said, standing behind her and wrapping his arms around her. She leaned back against him, rubbing her cheek against his springy beard and breathing in the scent of outdoors and freshly sawn wood that he'd brought with him.

"Beef stew," she said, "with noodles."

"My favorite," he said, giving her a squeeze before pulling away to hang up his coat and take off his heavy work boots and put on a pair of house shoes. Then he got himself a beer from the refrigerator and sat down at the kitchen table.

"How was work?" she asked. Bill was a restoration carpenter, and his latest project, converting an old root cellar into a wine cellar, was almost finished. He didn't have a new job lined up yet, and they were both a bit worried about it.

"Good news," he said, popping the top of his beer and taking a pull. "I might have a new job. Nothing definite, yet, but that Irish guy, Old Dan's brother, came by and asked me about renovating the Bilge. Seems he wants to fix it up."

Lucy's eyebrows shot up. "Already? The poor man's not even in his grave."

"Maybe they'd talked about it before Old Dan died," said Bill. "It seems like the plans are pretty well developed. This Dylan seems to know exactly what he wants, more than if he'd just walked in the door and decided the place needed some freshening up. He's talking about putting in a bay window and a fireplace and doing over the whole kitchen. It's going to be a real restaurant, not just a bar."

"So you think Dylan was coming in as a partner?"

Bill shrugged. "That's the impression I got. I know he wants to get started right away. He asked if I was available immediately, and I said I was."

"So you think you'll get the job?"

"I'm keeping my fingers crossed. The Bloomberg job is almost finished, and I don't have anything else lined up." He took a long swallow. "I'll work up the proposal tonight."

"Make it an offer he can't refuse," said Lucy. She managed the family budget and knew how tight things could get in the last months of winter, before building picked up again in the spring. She went over to the back stairway and yelled for Sara. "Supper's ready, and you haven't set the table. Let's go!"

There was no answer, but Lucy heard Sara clattering down the front stairs.

"What happened?" she asked Bill as she ladled the stew into the tureen. "When did my sweet, bouncy little Sara turn into this unpleasant stranger?"

"It's your fault," he said, a twinkle in his eye. "You kept feeding them, and they grew up."

"I've still got Zoe," she said, carrying the tureen into the dining room.

"But only for a few more years," warned Bill, following her with the noodles and salad. "She's growing up fast, too."

Later that night they had proof positive that Zoe was still very much a little girl. She woke in the middle of the night, sobbing hysterically and screaming for her parents.

"What's the matter?" asked Lucy, rushing to her bedside and taking her in her arms.

"I'm scared."

Lucy smoothed her daughter's damp hair. "There's nothing to be scared of. You're perfectly safe here, in your own bed, in your house, with your family all around."

"I know. But I'm still scared."

"You probably had a nightmare."

Zoe nodded.

"Do you remember what it was about?"

Zoe nodded again. "The h-h-headless man," she finally said.

"He can't hurt you," said Lucy, but she wasn't entirely convinced. It seemed that Tinker's Cove would be dealing with Old Dan's death for a long time to come, and in ways nobody quite expected.

Lucy remained with Zoe for almost an hour before the child fell back to sleep. Only then did she go back to her own bed, but she couldn't settle down. Her mind was full of stray thoughts: income tax, that shingle that blew off the roof, the funny noise the car was making. She finally did drift off but dreamt she was awake and wouldn't have believed she slept except for the fact that when the alarm went off at six, she rushed downstairs, convinced the dishwasher had overflowed on the kitchen floor. When she found the floor perfectly dry, she realized she must have been dreaming.

The girls had left for school minutes shy of missing the bus, Bill was in the shower, and she was still in her nightgown and robe, hanging on to her third mug of coffee at the kitchen table, when there was a knock at the door. She was surprised when she recognized Brian Donahue through the glass but figured he wanted to see Bill about some work.

"He's in the shower, but you're welcome to wait for him," she told him. "There's still some coffee in the pot if you'd like it."

"That would be great. Thanks," he said, taking off his hat and carefully wiping his boots on the mat.

"Take a seat," said Lucy, emptying the pot into a mug and setting it on the table in front of him. She sat back down and watched him add milk and sugar. "I hope you're not wasting your time. I don't think he's got any work coming up. Nothing for certain, that is."

Brian's eyebrows shot above his wire rims. "That's not what I heard. Dylan Malone told me he's hiring Bill to completely renovate the Bilge. 'Waterfront dining in summer and fireside dining in winter,' he said. 'With the atmosphere of a genuine Irish pub.' "

"Bill mentioned that last night, but he wasn't sure he had the job."

"Dylan seems to think he does."

"I guess he should know," said Lucy, with a smile.

"I could really use the work," said Brian. "Old Dan never paid me for a job I did a couple of months ago, fixing the rotted floor behind the bar." He swallowed some coffee, and his mouth twisted as if it were bitter, in spite of the four teaspoons of sugar he'd added. "That Old Dan sure was a cheap bastard. I never should've agreed to do the work unless he paid in advance. That's what everybody told me, but it was too late. I'd already finished the job." He raised his head and looked at her. "This is the only way I'll ever get a cent out of that cheapskate, if Bill hires me, you see?"

"You could go to the wake," she said. "Take your payment in free drinks."

"He owes me more than a couple of drinks," grumbled Brian.

"I've never been to a real Irish wake," said Lucy. "Just visiting hours at the funeral home."

"You think this'll be different?"

"I'm no expert, but from what I've heard, they're pretty lively affairs. Sometimes they even sit the dead person's body up and put a drink in its hand."

"That'd be a problem for Old Dan," said Brian, thoughtfully. "I mean, he could hold the drink, but you sort of need a head to complete the image. Not that he could actually drink it, of course, being dead and all, but you know what I mean."

Lucy did. How could you have a wake with a body that had no head?

The first thing Lucy noticed when she arrived at the Bilge for Old Dan's wake on Sunday afternoon was an unearthly noise, something between sobbing and moaning, which, she was surprised to discover, was issuing from Moira, who paused occasionally to dab at her dry eyes with a small, lace-trimmed linen handkerchief. To Lucy's relief, there was no sign of a body or even a closed coffin. Moira and her husband, both in black, were sitting side by side in front of the bar, where an enlarged photo of a much younger Old Dan was displayed. Candles were burning on either side of the photo, and a small bronze crucifix and a string of rosary beads had been arranged in front of it.

Only a handful of people had arrived so far, mostly elderly women, and they were seated in chairs that had been set against the wall, reciting the rosary with Father Ed. Lucy stood awkwardly in the doorway, unsure how to proceed. If this were visiting hours at the local funeral home, she would first have passed through a receiving line of mourners, and then, if the body was laid out in a casket, she would have paid her respects to the deceased. But here there was no receiving line, and she didn't feel comfortable interrupting Moira's vocal display of mourning. There was no sign of Deirdre, thank goodness, and Lucy assumed Moira had found somebody else to mind her.

She was greatly relieved when Frank Cahill approached her. "Thank you so much for coming," he said. "Would you like to express your sympathy to the family?"

"I'd like to, but I don't want to intrude," she replied. "Moira seems quite overcome with grief."

Frank shook his head. "No, no. She's keening. It's the expected thing, you see. She'd probably appreciate a break."

He stuck out his arm, rather like an usher at a wedding, and conducted Lucy to the bar, where he presented her to Dylan and Moira.

Moira fell silent and dabbed at her eyes, which were dry, and gave Lucy a small, tight smile.

"Lucy here wishes to tell you she's sorry for your trouble," prompted Frank.

"That's right. I'm very sorry. Terribly sorry," Lucy babbled, staring at the photo of Old Dan. It must have been his high school graduation picture, she thought, now that she had a closer view. It showed a cocky young man, with a thick head of red hair and a charming, lopsided grin.

"Did you know my brother well?" inquired Dylan. "It's a grand likeness, is it not?"

Lucy didn't think the photo looked anything like the Old Dan she'd known. The red hair had long ago turned to gray, and she couldn't recall ever seeing him smile. Mostly, he had kept his head down and muttered to himself on the rare occasions he'd left the Bilge to go to the bank or post office. While most people in town saw these necessary errands as an opportunity to chat and catch up on the news, Old Dan never greeted anyone, not even with a nod.

"He was a very handsome young man," said Lucy. "I really only had a nodding acquaintance with him."

"So you're here because of the paper? You're going to be writing up the wake?" asked Dylan.

"I sure am," said Lucy. "We've never had a traditional Irish wake here in town, and people will be interested."

"As well they might be," said Dylan. "We Irish are well acquainted with death and know a thing or two about sending a poor soul off in style. There's the keening, of course. Moira's a wonderful keener," said Dylan.

Moira blushed at the compliment. "And you see, we've turned the mirror to the wall," she said, pointing behind the bar.

"And stopped the clock," added Dylan, indicating a Guinness clock with its hands frozen at nine o'clock.

"And there's always plenty of food and drink at an Irish wake," said Father Ed, pointing to a lavish spread laid out on the bar's tables, which had been strung together and covered with a white linen cloth.

It was probably the first time in the Bilge's long and disreputable history that a tablecloth had been used, thought Lucy, noticing the platters of cold meats and steaming chafing dishes, with bottles of Irish whiskey liberally interspersed.

"Will you have a wee drop in memory of Old Dan?" asked Frank.

Lucy hesitated. She didn't really like whiskey, but there didn't seem to be anything else except Guinness stout, which she wasn't fond of, either. There was no sign of her preferred drink, white wine.

Frank gave her a nudge. "It's customary," he said, passing her a glass with a generous inch of amber liquid in the bottom.

"Well, then, here's to Old Dan," said Lucy, raising the glass and taking a sip.

"Now, now, that won't do," said Dylan, standing up and raising a glass. "May the road rise to meet you. May the wind be always at your back. May the sun shine warm upon your face, the rain fall soft upon your fields. And until we meet again . . ." he recited, pausing dramatically and lifting the glass higher, "may God hold you in the hollow of His hand." Then he drained his glass in one swallow and fixed his eyes on Lucy, challenging her to do the same.

"May God hold Old Dan in the hollow of his hand," she said and, taking a deep breath, downed the whiskey in her glass. "Now, if you'll excuse me, I think I'd better eat something right away, or this will go straight to my head."

"Absolutely, help yourself. There's plenty of everything and more where it came from," said Dylan.

Feeling slightly tipsy, Lucy made her way to the buffet. Once she had served herself, filling her plate with corned beef and cabbage and Irish soda bread, she took a seat and surveyed the room. People had been arriving steadily, and a good crowd had gathered, including a number of Old Dan's best customers. A few had even shaved and put on a clean shirt for the occasion. Frank conducted each person in turn to offer their sympathy to Dylan and Moira. Lucy chewed contentedly, interested in watching the people and listening to the occasional click of beads as the woman seated beside her quietly recited her Hail Marys and Our Fathers.

She was feeling quite mellow when the door flew open and Dave Reilly entered, his long hair streaming behind him. His jacket was open, revealing a T-shirt with the Claws logo, a lobster holding a guitar. Frank hurried over to greet him, but Dave shoved him aside and staggered drunkenly across the room, toward Dylan and Moira. Spotting him, Dylan immediately got to his feet and stood protectively in front of his wife.

"Here, now," said Dylan. "You're very welcome indeed if you want to pay your respects to my brother, but we don't want any trouble here."

"That's right," said Frank, taking hold of Dave's arm. "We don't want any trouble."

"Pay my respects!" bellowed Dave, shaking off Frank's hand and gesturing wildly with his arm. "That's a good one!" He stabbed his finger toward the photo of Old Dan. "He's the one who should pay me, and more than his respects. That old bastard owes me five thousand dollars, and I'm here to collect."

The room was suddenly silent. Even the old women had stopped mumbling their prayers.

"I'm afraid you've come to the wrong place," said Dylan, equably. "I never knew my brother to borrow money, him being rather tight with a dollar as I recall, but I don't doubt—"

"Borrow! He didn't borrow from me. He cheated me!" shouted Dave.

Dylan's face hardened, and he pulled himself to his full height. "You're saying my brother was a cheat?" he asked, puffing out his chest.

"A damned rotten cheater, that's what he was," said Dave, tossing his hair back and clenching his fist. "I bought a winning lottery ticket off him. It was worth five thousand dollars, but when I gave it to him for payment, he told me it was no good, that I had it wrong. And I believed him!"

"Anyone can make a mistake," said Dylan, with a shrug.

"It was no mistake," said Dave. "I had the winning ticket, but he switched it on me, and a week later I hear he's been to the lottery commission to collect the money."

"It seems to me that's water under the bridge," said Frank. "Whoever's got the ticket wins the money."

"And what do you want me to do about it?" asked Dylan.

"I want you to pay me, that's what. I want my five thousand dollars!" Dave lowered his voice to a threatening growl. "And I'm not leaving until I get it."

Dylan shook his head. "I haven't got it, so I can't give it to you, can I?"

"Oh, it's here all right," said Dave, marching around the bar and yanking open a drawer. "The old miser stashed everything away." He was working his way along the bar, pulling open drawers and dumping their contents on the floor. Coins and bottle caps were rolling every which way; bits of paper and string and plastic bags all came tumbling out.

"That's enough, now," said Dylan. "This isn't the time or the place."

"Oh, it isn't?" said Dave, whirling around. He lifted his

arm and socked Dylan right on the jaw, making a sicken-
ing smacking noise as his fist connected with Dylan's face.

From the sound, Lucy expected Dylan to crumple to the
floor, but he remained on his feet. He gave his head a quick
shake, worked his jaw from side to side, and then, taking
Dave unawares, caught him with a left hook. Dave responded by trying to wrap his hands around Dylan's neck,
a move that Dylan blocked by wrapping his arms around
Dave and pinning his arms to his sides. The two men staggered around the room like exhausted boxers, smashing
into chairs and tables and scattering the assembled mourners, most of whom were watching the fight avidly, including the ladies with rosaries. The Bilge regulars were more
vocal, delivering cheers when a punch connected and jeer-
ing at the misses. It wasn't until the combatants threatened
to tumble into the refreshments that Father Ed decided it
was time to intervene.

"Break it up," he said, grabbing each man by the shoulder and pulling them apart. "If you've got to have a fight,
take it outside, but don't be knocking over the Jameson
whiskey. Don't you know it's sacrilege?"

"Right, Father, right," panted Dylan. "I shouldn't be
fighting at my own brother's wake."

"And you," said Father Ed, pointing a finger at Dave.
"You should be ashamed of yourself. Now get yourself out
of here, and I expect to see you at confession tonight and
at mass bright and early tomorrow morning."

Dave hung his head. "Yes, Father."

"Now be off with you," said Father Ed, shooing Dave
out the door. When it closed behind him, Father Ed turned
to the group. "It wouldn't be a real Irish wake without a
bit of a dustup, now would it?" he asked, and a number of
people chuckled in agreement and began setting the room
to rights. Frank produced a fiddle and began tuning it,
soon producing a lively jig.

When he'd finished, Moira asked him to play "Danny

Boy" for her, and she sang so beautifully that a couple of the old ladies had to dry their eyes. Other songs followed, and soon everybody was joining in, singing old tunes their mothers and aunts and fathers and uncles had sung to them. Lucy had never seen anything like it. This wasn't like the formal recitals she was used to: it was simply a group of people joining together to sing the songs they loved. She recognized some of them, she even knew the words to a few, but for the most part, she just sat and listened until she realized it was getting late and she had to get home to make dinner. She dragged herself away, straining to hear the last bits of music as she crossed the parking lot to her car.

Chapter Six

"I hear that wake was something else," declared Phyllis when Lucy arrived at work on Monday morning. "Elfrida says there was a real hootenanny with fiddle music and singing."

"Was she there? I didn't see her," said Lucy.

"Was she there? Are you kidding?" snorted Phyllis. "That one wouldn't pass up a free meal."

"There was plenty of food. And drink, too."

"Well, one thing I will say for Elfrida," said Phyllis, smoothing her sweater—a black cardigan trimmed with a tasteful scattering of jet beads—over her still substantial but somewhat deflated bosom, "she's a teetotaler. Won't touch a drop of alcohol. Not since her first husband died in that crash. Drunk as a skunk."

"Elfrida certainly has had an interesting life," said Lucy.

"You can say that again," agreed Phyllis. "She's on her fourth husband, and to tell the truth, I don't think he's going to last much longer."

"Is he sick?"

"Strong as an ox. And a good provider, too. But Elfrida says he's boring."

"You can't have everything."

"That's what I keep telling her, but she says stability isn't everything. She needs more, she says."

"It seems to me that having six kids would be exciting enough for anyone," observed Lucy, sitting down at her desk.

"Didn't I tell you? She's pregnant again."

"She's a one-person population boom," said Lucy.

"If you ask me, she should figure out what causes it and stop doing it," sniffed Phyllis. "The IGA's too crowded by far these days. And the traffic . . ."

Lucy smiled to herself as she booted up the computer. "You can't blame it all on Elfrida. And it works the other way, too. We've printed quite a few obits lately." She sighed. "I'll be darned if I know what I'm going to write about Old Dan."

"Might as well save yourself the trouble," said Phyllis. "Everybody's heard all about it already."

"Somehow I don't think that's quite the attitude Ted's looking for," said Lucy as the door flew open and Ted breezed in.

"What attitude would that be?" he demanded, unzipping his jacket and tossing it at the coat rack, where it caught on a hook.

"All the news that's fit to print and some that isn't," said Phyllis, smiling smugly. "That's what I was telling Lucy."

"And what's wrong with that?" he asked.

"Nothing," said Lucy, finding herself on the spot and not liking it very much. "We were just joking."

"Oh." He shrugged and sat down at his desk. "I heard that wake was pretty rowdy. I'd like to put it on the front page. Did you get any pictures?"

"I think so," said Lucy. "I snapped a nice one of Frank Cahill playing the fiddle."

"Fiddles at funerals? What next?" said Ted.

"It sure beats sitting around in the funeral parlor," said Phyllis. "And Elfrida said the food was a lot better than the sherry and peanut butter and bacon hors d'oeuvres you usually get at the reception afterwards."

"It was not the usual Tinker's Cove funeral," agreed Lucy, typing in the phrase as the lead for her story. Her fingers flew over the keyboard as the story seemed to write itself. When she finished, she turned to Ted. "Any news on the investigation?"

He shook his head. "The police have been interviewing Bilge regulars, but they're not making much progress. That bunch isn't real comfortable talking to the cops."

"Guilty consciences, no doubt," said Phyllis.

"You got it," said Ted. "Though there's a big difference between taking an undersized lobster now and then and slicing off somebody's head. I don't really see one of the regulars as the murderer."

"Little grudges can get out of hand," said Lucy, "and a lot of people had bones to pick with Old Dan."

"Anybody in particular?" asked Ted.

"As a matter of fact, yes. Dave Reilly, you know that kid who plays with the Claws, he was complaining at the wake that Old Dan gypped him out of a winning lottery ticket. He came to blows with Dylan about it."

"Probably just had a little too much of that free booze," said Ted.

"Well, yeah," said Lucy. "What do you think those guys do all day at the Bilge? They drink. Old Dan was always willing to pour another. He never cut anybody off that I ever heard of."

"Me, neither," said Phyllis, clucking her tongue. "Too much drink can bring out the devil in any man."

"And Dave Reilly's not the only one," continued Lucy. "Brian Donahue's been moaning around town about how Old Dan stiffed him on money he owed him for some re-pairs."

"Makes you wonder how big a tab Brian had run up," said Ted. "Old Dan probably figured they were even."

"Not according to Brian," said Lucy. "But that's not really the point I'm trying to make. Just think. I never set foot in the Bilge until the wake, but if I can think of two people who had grudges against Old Dan, there must be a heck of a lot more who have really big chips on their shoulders."

"Wouldn't surprise me," said Phyllis.

"I dunno," said Ted. "I think Old Dan could have been into something outside of Tinker's Cove. Like organized crime, the IRA, something like that."

"You've been watching *The Sopranos* again, haven't you?" accused Phyllis.

"Actually, yes," replied Ted. "But the fact that he was beheaded doesn't seem to fit with some drunk fisherman. It's more like somebody is sending a message."

"Somebody very evil," said Lucy, shivering.

"You guys are giving me the creeps," said Phyllis.

An hour or two later, Lucy found herself on the town beach, wishing she'd worn warmer clothes. She'd been fooled by the blue sky and bright February sunshine into thinking it was warmer than it actually was. A stiff northerly breeze was blowing across the water, whipping up whitecaps and tossing her hair, working its way up her coat sleeves and down her collar. On days like this, she couldn't imagine what it would be like to be a fisherman out on the open sea. Maybe the physical work kept them warm, maybe they got used to it, but she was already thinking about retreating to the warmth of her car when she spotted her quarry. Shoving her hands deeper into her pockets, she struggled across the loose gravel, toward the lone metal prospector out today.

"Hi!" she hailed him. "Do you have a minute?"

"I've got all the time in the world," he replied, slowly swinging the wand of his metal detector back and forth across the pebbles.

Unlike her, the prospector was dressed for the weather

in an olive green army surplus parka with a fur-trimmed hood. Underneath the hood, she discovered he was well into his sixties, with bushy gray eyebrows, blue eyes, and red cheeks and nose. He was also wearing insulated pants and sturdy rubber boots.

"I'm Lucy Stone, from the *Pennysaver*. I'm writing a story about prospectors like yourself, and I'd like to ask you a few questions, if you don't mind."

"I don't mind. I could use the company. It gets a bit lonely out here," he said, extending his mittened hand. "Paul Sullivan's the name."

"Not too many people on the beach this time of year, are there?" said Lucy, taking his hand. "So tell me, what exactly are you looking for?"

"The pot of gold at the end of the rainbow," said Paul, winking at her. "But until I find it, I'll take whatever turns up. Rings and jewelry that people wore to the beach in the summer. Coins that fell out of their pockets. Doubloons washed up from sunken pirate ships . . ."

"Really?"

"Not yet," said Paul, with a shrug, "but you never know."

"What's the most interesting thing you've found?"

"A little brass plate from a ship, with the words *life jackets* inscribed on it. I've always wondered what ship it came from and how it happened to sink."

This was pretty good stuff, thought Lucy, scribbling away in her notebook. "And the most valuable?"

"A diamond ring."

"You're kidding!"

"No. Two carats. I had it appraised. They said it was worth seven thousand dollars."

Lucy thought of the little half-carat solitaire engagement ring she was wearing on her finger. She never wore it when she went swimming or worked in the garden, but always placed it carefully on the crystal ring holder sitting on her dresser. "Some poor woman must have been awfully upset when she discovered she'd lost it," she said.

"Finders keepers, losers weepers," said Paul, winking again.

"You didn't advertise for the owner? They might've given you a reward."

"Or they might not," said Paul. "I decided to play it safe and kept the ring."

"Do you still have it?"

He shook his head. "All I've got is the Social Security, you see. The little bit I make from prospecting helps keep a roof above me head. So I sold it so I'd have something against a rainy day—or an empty oil tank."

Lucy felt a surge of sympathy, tinged with fear for her own future. Chamberlain College was making fast work of the education fund, and there was no retirement fund at all for her and Bill. "On average, how much do you think you make in a year?" she asked.

"On average? I don't know. I certainly don't find a diamond ring every day, you know. And I didn't get seven thousand, only about half that. So I guess, on average I make a couple of thousand a year."

Lucy nodded. "It's a lot of work, too, I imagine."

"Ah, but there's the health benefits. Plenty of fresh air and exercise—if I don't catch me death of the pneumonia."

By now it was blowing harder, and Lucy's teeth were chattering. It was time to wind this interview up. "Well, thanks so much for your time. Do you mind if I take your picture for the paper?"

"Ah, better not. My ugly mug might break your camera."

"Oh, I've heard that line before," said Lucy, who was used to coaxing people to pose. "It won't hurt a bit. I promise."

But Paul Sullivan was having none of it. "No, no. I must

insist," he said firmly. "But I did see a couple of other prospectors down around the bend. Perhaps you could photograph them."

"Thanks for the tip," said Lucy, watching as he continued on his way across the beach, swinging the metal detector as he went. She cast a longing glance at the Subaru, which she knew would be toasty warm from sitting in the sun, and began trudging across the pebbly beach in the direction he'd indicated. It was tough going. She was walking against the wind, and her favorite slip-on driving shoes were too flexible to offer support on the slippery gravel. She finally reached the rock breakwater that sheltered the swimming area and clambered up onto the boulders to get a better view, but there was no sign of anyone on the beach. She must have missed them, she decided, pulling her beret down over her ears and shoving her hands in her pockets for the trek back. Or maybe they were never there at all, she thought, wondering if Paul Sullivan had sent her on a wild goose chase to avoid having his picture taken.

Back in the warm car, she rubbed her frozen hands together and tried to relax the muscles that had clenched against the cold, but she was seized with fits of shivering. When her hands had thawed enough to grip the steering wheel, she started the engine and drove slowly across the parking lot, which was empty except for a few seagulls, which waited until the car was almost upon them before walking out of the way. They didn't consider her enough of a threat to bother flying.

Unlike the gulls, Lucy didn't have the luxury of sitting in the sun. She was already late for a planning board meeting, and they were taking a vote on the first agenda item when she arrived.

"The board votes four to one to approve a site plan for six additional parking spaces at the Seaman's Cooperative

Bank," said Chairman Ralph Nickerson, with a bang of his gavel.

"Thank you very much," said the architect, rolling up the plans, which had been spread on a table in front of the board members.

"That goes for me, too," said the bank president, shaking hands with each board member in turn.

"Next on the agenda, we have an application from Dylan and Daniel Malone for improvements to the façade of the Bilge, located at 15B Main Street, book two, page one twenty-three," said Nickerson. "Are the applicants present?"

Dylan Malone stood up. "I am Dylan Malone," he said, his brogue rather thicker than usual. "As you have probably heard, my brother, Daniel, is now deceased."

"We extend our sympathies to you, Mr. Malone," said Nickerson. The board members nodded in agreement. "I assume you wish to go forward with the application?"

"Yes, I do," said Dylan, stepping forward and distributing copies of the plans to each member. "As the surviving partner, I am now the sole owner. My brother and I . . ." Here Dylan's voice broke, and he took a moment to collect himself before continuing. "My brother and I had hoped to undertake a complete remodeling of the bar, transforming it into a full-service restaurant offering waterfront dining in the summer and fireside dining in winter. As I understand the situation, this board only has oversight of the exterior changes."

"That is correct," said Nickerson.

"Well, as you can see, the plans call for new clapboard siding, a new door in a traditional style, and the installation of a bow window with flower boxes. In addition, the area immediately in front of the building will be surfaced with flagstone and fenced off, creating a patio."

This was a major improvement, thought Lucy, recalling the Bilge's dingy appearance, which featured dark, rotting

cedar shingles; a single small window, which was cur-
tained in black cloth; and a somewhat scarred and dented
steel door. It was distinctly unwelcoming, sending the message that if you weren't a regular, you had no business
going there.

"And will there be tables on the patio in the warmer
months?" asked Millicent Fenton, one of the board members. She had snow-white hair piled on her head and a
string of pearls around her neck and spoke with the perfect diction of a private girls' school graduate circa 1950.

"I would like to have that option, yes," said Dylan. "In
the summer people enjoy eating outside in the fresh sea air
and sunshine."

"Yes, they do," said Millicent, beaming at him.

Lucy would have been willing to bet the house that this
proposal would pass easily. The Bilge had been an eyesore
for as long as anyone could remember, and the board
members weren't going to pass up an opportunity to get
rid of it.

"Is there any comment from the public?" asked Nickerson, rhetorically. He seemed surprised when one of the
handful of people in the audience raised his hand.

"Uh, yes, would you state your name and address please?"
said Nickerson.

"I'm Will Gottsegen, and I live at Thirty-five Exchange
Street."

"That's an apartment building, isn't it?" asked Nickerson, looking down his nose and over his half-glasses. "Are
you a renter?"

"It's my building, and I'm here about some improvements I want to make," said Gottsegen, who was wearing
jeans and the rubber boots favored by fishermen. "But I'd
like to make a comment about these plans for the Bilge. It
sounds to me like it's going to get too fancy for the local
folk, if you know what I mean. We've got plenty of places

in town for the tourists, but what about us working folk? Where are we supposed to go? The Bilge is more than a bar. It's a place where a working man can relax after a hard day, and it don't seem like a guy who's been sweating and baiting traps all day is gonna be welcome there anymore."

"Everyone will be welcome," proclaimed Dylan. "Of that, you can be sure. It will be like a real Irish pub, where the whole community can gather for refreshment."

Gottsegen grimaced, clearly skeptical of Dylan's claim, but the board members nodded, clearly entranced with the idea of an Irish pub in Tinker's Cove.

"And will there be entertainment? Will your lovely wife sing those charming Irish tunes she sang at the wake?" asked Nickerson.

"Yes, indeed," said Dylan. "There will be entertainment, genuine Irish sessions, and I'm sure my Moira will be joining in from time to time."

"Ah, that will be fine," said Nickerson. "Shall we vote?"

As Lucy recorded the vote, which was unanimously in favor, it occurred to her that the wake had been perfectly timed to convince the board of the desirability of transforming the Bilge into an upscale establishment. The application had been submitted before Old Dan's death and had his name on it, but she doubted that the improvements were his idea. He had been content for as long as anyone could remember to cater to the local working crowd. She'd never heard even a whisper that changes were in store for the Bilge. And, looking at Gottsegen's scowling face, she was pretty sure it was unwelcome news to him and the other regulars.

Dylan, on the other hand, was beaming as he shook hands with each of the board members and thanked them. It occurred to Lucy that Dylan was behaving as if he intended to settle in Tinker's Cove, so she followed him out of the meeting room and caught him in the hall.

"Do you mind answering a few follow-up questions?" she asked, with a friendly smile.

"I'm in an awful hurry," he said, tossing his scarf over his shoulder.

"I'll make it quick," she said. "As you heard tonight, a lot of Old Dan's regular customers never guessed that he was planning to upgrade the Bilge and are quite upset. Was it really his idea?"

Dylan didn't miss a beat but threw her a grin. "My brother tended to keep his cards close to his chest, if you know what I mean."

"So the plan was for you and your family to relocate to Tinker's Cove so you could become an active partner in the business?"

"You know we Irish aren't much for the long-range plan. We tend to take things as they come." Dylan shrugged. "Now I really must go, or my Moira will be fretting and wondering what's keeping me."

"Well, thanks for your time," said Lucy, heading back to the meeting room and retaking her seat. She tried to keep her mind on the topic at hand—a request from the Community Church to replace its traditional wooden shingles with asphalt, which was prompting a heated discussion—but her thoughts kept returning to Old Dan's murder. She knew that prosecutors always kept in mind the Latin phrase *cui bono*, which she understood meant "who benefits," when investigating a crime, and it seemed that Dylan had come to town with plans for his inheritance. Of course, he had an alibi, because he hadn't arrived in town until after the murder, but that didn't mean he couldn't have had a hand in arranging Old Dan's death. Was ownership of the Bilge, not to mention Old Dan's house and whatever other assets he might have stashed away, a strong enough motive to commit murder? Maybe, she thought, for an aging actor whose career had stalled.

After all, Dylan would hardly have taken the job directing an amateur production if he had had a more promising alternative.

"Well, I guess we're done for tonight," said the committee chairman, banging his gavel.

Lucy felt her face reddening. "Sorry," she said, raising her hand. "What was that vote?"

Chapter Seven

It was one thing to enjoy going to the theater for an evening out and another thing entirely to actually get on stage and perform, thought Lucy as she drove over to Miss Tilley's house to pick up Rachel on Saturday morning. It was audition day, and Lucy had serious doubts about the whole thing. She couldn't imagine why she'd let Rachel convince her to try out for the show. No, she'd be happy to buy tickets for the whole family and sit in the audience and clap like crazy for the local amateurs, but get on stage herself? Impossible!

No, she told herself, the only reason she was even going to the audition was because she'd promised Rachel, and maybe, she admitted to herself, to get a look at Dylan in action and consider whether he really was a likely suspect in his brother's murder.

Rachel was at the door of Miss Tilley's little gray-shingled, Cape Cod–style cottage when Lucy pulled into the driveway, and she called to Lucy when she got out of the car. "Come on in. Miss T wants to visit with you."

Lucy was pleased at the prospect of catching up with her old friend, especially if it meant delaying her moment of truth at the audition. Julia Ward Howe Tilley—nobody called her anything except Miss Tilley—was the town's oldest resident and was long retired from her job as town librarian. It was in that capacity that Lucy first met her, soon after she and Bill and baby Toby had arrived in Tinker's Cove and settled in their "handyman's special" on Red Top Road. Lucy treasured her friendship but knew it couldn't go on forever, since Miss T was well over ninety. She had lost none of her sharp wit, however, although she did rely on Rachel for help with daily chores, like cooking and cleaning.

"Well, Lucy Stone! It's about time you paid a visit to a decrepit old lady," said Miss Tilley, grasping Lucy's hands with hers and giving them a strong squeeze.

"Not that decrepit, if your hand strength is any indication," said Lucy, stretching out her fingers. "How are you? Still doing yoga every morning?"

"Of course," said the old woman, pointing to a chair. "Sit down and stay awhile. I want to hear all about Dan Malone's gruesome end."

"Not much to tell, really," said Lucy, unbuttoning her coat and perching on the chair. "They found him in the harbor, without his head. That's all anybody knows so far."

"I never thought much of him," sniffed Miss Tilley. "No better than Paddy's pig he was."

Seeing Rachel's raised eyebrows, Miss Tilley adopted a stubborn expression and defended her choice of words. "That's what my father used to say. He didn't think much of the Irish, and he wasn't alone. And now we're practically being invaded, what with this brother and his wife and even a child. The town's being overrun. *Finian's Rainbow* for goodness sake. Why put on that old chestnut when they could go with something trendy, like *Hair*."

Hearing this, Lucy began to giggle, and Miss Tilley fixed her with a beady stare. "It's just because it's Irish. That's the only reason they're doing it," she said.

"Maybe the church preferred a show that didn't include nudity," said Lucy.

"Well, the church was founded by Irish immigrants," said Rachel. "They're celebrating its hundred-year anniversary."

"Don't remind me," said Miss Tilley. "One hundred years of papist nonsense! Fish on Friday and people wearing nasty smudges on their foreheads on Ash Wednesday and those enormous families because they're not allowed to use birth control, all because some silly old man in Rome said they'd go to hell, as if he knew anything about the difficulties of producing and raising a family!"

"Things have changed quite a bit," said Lucy, amused at the old spinster's vehemence on the subject. "Nowadays most Catholics practice birth control."

"And about time, too," said Miss Tilley. "Why it was tragic what those young girls went through. Why Old Dan's mother herself got in trouble. That's why she had to leave her job here and go back to Ireland."

This was news to Lucy. "Old Dan's mother lived here? In Tinker's Cove?"

"Indeed she did. I remember her well. Brigid Heaney was her name. She worked for my mother as a maid of all work. . . ."

"When was this?" asked Lucy.

"Oh, let me see, it was before the Second World War, of course. It was when Mama's health began to fail. The late thirties, around then, I think, and Mama was very glad to have the help, but she quit after a few months and went to work for the O'Donnells. Better pay, she claimed, and she wouldn't have to work so hard since she was only going to have to clean house and wouldn't have to do the laundry and help with the cooking, like she did for Mother."

"You mean the ambassador, Mick O'Donnell?" asked Lucy, naming the founder of a legendary political dynasty that continued to the present day. Lieutenant Governor Cormac O'Donnell still occasionally used the enormous Queen Anne–style family "cottage" on Shore Road.

"He was just a congressman then," said Miss Tilley,

with a sniff. "And she was only with them for a year or so before she hightailed it back to Ireland in a hurry to get married to Mr. Malone." She chuckled. "We got the birth announcement seven months later."

"She was lucky to have that option," said Rachel. "A lot of girls in her situation found themselves out on the street, with no choice but to become prostitutes."

"Not little Brigid. She knew how to take care of herself. That's for sure. She might've been on her hands and knees scrubbing the floor, but she'd tell you she was descended from the High Kings of Ireland, that her situation was only a small setback," said Miss Tilley, leaning back and slapping her hands on her bony thighs. "She had the gift of blarney. That's for sure!"

"So who was the father of Brigid's child?" asked Lucy, scenting a scandal. "Was it the ambassador?"

"I wouldn't put it past him, but there were plenty of other lads about," said Miss Tilley. "I imagine she managed to convince the poor fellow she married that it was his, come a bit early. That's what girls did then. Or maybe the ambassador gave her some money, to sweeten the deal."

Lucy and Rachel sat silently for a minute, reflecting on the advantages of coming of age after the invention of the birth control pill. Then Rachel roused herself and checked her watch.

"We'd better get going, Lucy, or we'll miss the audition."

"That would be fine with me," said Lucy. "I'd be perfectly happy painting scenery."

Rachel grabbed Lucy's hand and pulled her out of the chair. "Come on! Since when have you been a shrinking violet?"

"Since I heard singing was required," said Lucy, laughing.

"Break a leg, girls!" called Miss Tilley as they hurried out the door.

Lucy and Rachel had a hard time finding a parking space near the church and weren't surprised when they found the church hall packed with people. It seemed that everybody wanted a chance to stand in the spotlight and be in the show, and it took quite a few minutes before they spotted Pam in the crowd.

"I blame *American Idol*," said Lucy, greeting Pam with a hug. "Everybody wants to be a star."

"We shouldn't have to wait long," said Pam. "I put all our names in together. I think we'll be called any minute now."

"So what's the drill?" asked Lucy, surveying the chaotic scene. There seemed to be no rhyme or reason to the audition. Everybody just seemed to be waiting, except for Frank Cahill, who was seated at the piano, and Dylan and Moira, who were standing on the stage, deep in discussion. Little Deirdre, Lucy noticed, was sitting all by herself in a corner, absorbed in a book.

"You just put your name on the sign-up sheet and wait to be called," said Pam. "Shh, I think I hear my name. Come on."

She dashed ahead, wiggling her way through the crowd, followed by Lucy and Rachel, and was already singing "Look to the Rainbow" for Frank when they caught up with her at the piano.

"Fine, fine," he said after a few bars. "I'm sure we can use you in the chorus."

Pam clapped her hands together. "Great."

Then it was Rachel's turn to try out, and Frank handed her a piece of sheet music. She hardly looked at it, and didn't wait for Frank to cue her, but simply started singing the song, which she knew by heart, in her clear, lovely voice.

The crowded room fell silent as she worked her way through the lyrics, not even pausing for breath before the high notes.

When she finished, there was a smattering of applause, and she blushed, embarrassed.

Frank looked thoughtful as he asked, "Could you do a bit of 'How Are Things in Glocca Morra?' "

"Sure," said Rachel, promptly reeling off that song, too. As Lucy listened to the lyrics, an idyllic Irish landscape developed in her mind, complete with green fields, chirping birds, and charming thatched cottages.

This time everybody clapped when Rachel finished, and there were a few whistles and cheers.

"You obviously know this show," said Frank.

"I played Sharon in a college production," admitted Rachel.

"Do you think you could handle a leading part now?" he asked.

Rachel's face lit up. "I'm sure I could."

But before Frank could continue, Dylan was at his side. "Could I have a word, Frank?" he asked.

Frank followed him a few steps away, and they watched as a spirited discussion ensued. There was much waving of hands and shaking of heads, but in the end Dylan seemed to carry the argument, and Frank returned to the piano, with a glum expression.

"Well, Rachel, it seems we already have a Sharon," he said. "You could be in the chorus and understudy for La Malone." He rolled his eyes as he said the name. "Moira there will be Sharon, or you could have the part of Susan. That is, if you can dance."

Rachel shook her head. "Not well enough to play Susan," she said. "I'm thrilled to be in the chorus. That's fine with me."

"Right," said Frank, obviously unhappy. He shot a dark look at the stage, where Dylan and Moira had their heads together over the script, and growled, "Who's next? Lucy Stone!"

Here goes nothing, thought Lucy, stepping forward.

"I didn't know our star reporter could sing," he said, recognizing her.

"I'm going to try," said Lucy.

He played the introduction. She took a deep breath and managed to croak out a few lines of "Look to the Rainbow." When she got to the high notes, she gave up, with an embarrassed shrug.

"You're obviously not a singer," he said. "But I do need altos. Let's try a lower register."

Lucy managed a bit better with the alto part, but Frank was clearly unimpressed. "I'm going to put you down as a maybe," he said.

Lucy nodded in agreement, relieved to be off the hook, but Rachel and Pam protested. Their raised voices attracted Moira's attention, and she hurried over, script in hand.

"Lucy! It's great to see you here!" said Moira as she wrapped her arm around Lucy's shoulders and tossed her flaming curls back over her shoulder. "Lucy's my great friend, Frank," she said pointedly. "I'm sure she'll be a wonderful addition to the show."

Frank hung his head, hit a few chords on the piano, and slowly raised his head, meeting Moira's gaze, with a shrug. "Okay. Whatever. You're in, Lucy."

Pam and Rachel squealed in delight and wrapped themselves around Lucy and Moira, and soon they were all shrieking and jumping up and down like teenyboppers at a pop concert. But even as she made an outward show of delight at being included in the show, Lucy had her doubts. She suspected Moira saw her role more as baby-sitter than performer.

Those suspicions were confirmed when Moira was distributing scripts to the cast members and paused to have a word with Lucy. "And what's your darling little Zoe doing today?" she asked. "Poor Deirdre's been stuck here for hours, and I know she's missing her friends from home."

"I saw her there in the corner," said Lucy. "I'm sure Zoe would love to have a playmate this afternoon. Shall I take her home with me now?"

"That would be wonderful, Lucy," said Moira, all smiles. "I'll get her coat."

"Now I call that a smooth operator," said Pam.

"I always feel foolish when I meet a manipulative woman like that," confessed Rachel. "Why do I feel that I have to do everything myself?"

"It's no big deal," said Lucy, defensively. "Zoe and Deirdre get along really well. Sometimes it's easier to have another kid in the house. Zoe will be too busy to bother me, and I'll be able to cook dinner in peace."

"Right," said Pam as Moira approached, holding Zoe's pink parka and Hello Kitty backpack, which she handed to Lucy before disappearing in a swirl of black skirt.

"And denial is a river in Egypt," said Rachel, watching as Lucy bent down to zip the little girl's parka.

The girls had a point, admitted Lucy as she drove home with Deirdre safely buckled into the backseat, but the child wasn't a bit of trouble. She sat quietly, looking out the window and crooning a little song to herself.

"What are you singing?" asked Lucy.

"A fairy song," said Deirdre.

"You made it up yourself then?" asked Lucy.

"No, I didn't make it up," said Deirdre. "A fairy taught it to me."

"Ah," said Lucy, smiling to herself. What an imagination this kid had. She turned on the radio, hoping to catch the weather report, but instead heard the announcer saying that the medical examiner's report on the Tinker's

Cove beheading had been released and quickly switched it off. There was no sense fueling an overactive little mind like Deirdre's.

As she expected, Zoe was thrilled when Lucy arrived with Deirdre in tow, and the two immediately ran off to play together in Zoe's room. When Lucy brought them a lunch of peanut butter sandwiches and apple juice, she found them busily transforming some of Zoe's Barbie dolls into fairies.

"Mom, what can we use for wings?" asked Zoe, shoving the straw into her drink box.

Deirdre didn't seem to know what to do with the drink box, so Lucy helped her, showing her how to pull off the straw and insert it into the little hole. Maybe they didn't have them in Ireland, mused Lucy, taking a mental inventory of her sewing box. Coming up empty there, she turned to her collection of wrapping paper and ribbon.

"Tissue paper?" suggested Lucy. "I have some wide Christmas ribbon. It's gold."

"Silver would be better," said Deirdre.

"Let's take a look," said Lucy.

They followed her into her bedroom, where she opened the trunk at the foot of the bed and found the shoe box she used for odd bits of ribbon. When she left them, they were kneeling on the floor, happily examining the various scraps salvaged from birthdays and Christmases past.

Back in the kitchen, Lucy was rinsing beans for a pot of soup when she remembered the autopsy results, and she called Ted at the newspaper office. She knew he'd probably be there, even though it was Saturday.

"I hear you're going to be in the show," said Ted. "I didn't know you could sing and dance."

"I can't," admitted Lucy. "But I can baby-sit the star's daughter."

"Ah," said Ted. "It's like that, is it?"

"I really don't mind. Deirdre's a sweetheart. And it's not like I have to sing by myself. I can blend in with everybody else. I hope."

"I'm sure you'll be fine," he said, chuckling. "Pam says it's going to be terrific."

"I don't know about terrific. Maybe interesting is more like it. Listen, Ted, the reason I called is I wonder if you've heard about the autopsy?"

"Talk about interesting," he said. "The beheading was expertly done by someone with a sharp blade and a good bit of strength. And Old Dan was dead before he was beheaded."

"Do they know how he died?"

"Whatever it was, it happened to his head. There was nothing the matter with his body except a little liver damage. Not enough to kill him. No bullet holes, no trauma, nothing. So whatever it was—a bullet, a blow, a tumor—it was in his head."

"And they haven't found the head?"

"No, and they may never find it if it's in the bottom of the bay. But the police are assuming his death was not natural. . . ."

"Good thinking," said Lucy.

"And they're continuing to investigate," finished Ted.

Just then the girls came into the kitchen, eager to show Lucy how they'd transformed the Barbies into fairies.

"I've gotta go, Ted," she said, ending the call and examining the girls' handiwork.

They'd dressed the dolls in Barbie's sheerest nighties, the ruffled baby dolls, and had carefully stitched loops of ribbon to the backs to create colorful wings.

"Those are great," enthused Lucy. "They look like they could really fly."

"All fairies can fly," said Deirdre.

"Of course, they can," said Lucy. She was beginning to be a little disturbed by Deirdre's unwavering belief in otherworldly creatures and couldn't help adding a cautionary warning. "Maybe fairies can fly, but you're not a fairy. You're a human girl," said Lucy, "and humans can't fly. Right?"

"I flew in an airplane," said Deirdre.

"Right. Humans can fly in airplanes and helicopters, but even if they put on wings, they can't fly like fairies can."

"Mommy and I pretended we were fairies when we were in the airplane. We flew through the clouds," replied Deirdre.

"That must have been fun," said Lucy, joining in the make-believe. "And what about Daddy? Did he fly through the clouds, too, like the king of the fairies?"

"I don't know," said Deirdre. "He wasn't with us."

"He sat in another part of the plane?" asked Lucy, suddenly interested.

"No. He was on another plane. He left before us."

"The same day?" asked Lucy.

"No. Mommy and I went to Gram's after he left, for a visit. Then we put on our fairy wings and flew to America, where he was waiting for us."

My, my, wasn't this interesting, thought Lucy, who had assumed the family arrived together. But if Dylan had indeed arrived earlier, she realized, he didn't have an alibi, and he couldn't be excluded as a suspect. It wasn't a pleasant thought, especially since he had a wife and child, and she hoped he wasn't the murderer. She smiled at Deirdre, who was making her Barbie swoop through the air.

"Just remember," said Lucy, recalling stories she'd heard of children jumping off roofs, under the impression they were superheroes, "fairy wings only work inside airplanes."

"C'mon, Deirdre," said Zoe, taking her friend's hand. "Let's go back upstairs and make a house for the fairies."

The two little girls had started up the stairs together when there was a tap at the kitchen door.

"It's Molly!" shrieked Zoe, dropping Deirdre's hand and skipping across the kitchen. "Molly's here!"

"Hi, Zoe," said Molly, closing the door behind her. "Who's your friend?"

"This is Deirdre. She's from Ireland," said Zoe.

"It's nice to meet you, Deirdre," said Molly, extending her hand in greeting to Deirdre, who took it and gave a polite shake.

"Molly is my brother Toby's girlfriend," said Zoe. "They're going to have a baby."

Lucy dumped the beans into a pot and set it on the stove. "You girls go on and play now," she said. "Molly and I want to visit." She pulled a chair out from under the table and turned to Molly, eying her bulging tummy. "Take a load off your feet."

"Oh, I can't stay. I just came to borrow some molasses. If you have any, that is."

"I bought some at Christmas, for cookies," said Lucy, dragging the step stool over to a corner cupboard. She climbed up and began shifting jars and cans around on the shelves.

"I have the worst yen for molasses cookies," said Molly, easing into the chair and rubbing her stomach.

Deirdre remained in the kitchen despite Zoe's tugs, staring at Molly. "Does it hurt to have a baby inside you?" she asked.

Molly laughed. "No. It doesn't hurt to have it inside. It's getting it out that hurts. At least, that's what I hear. I never had a baby before."

Lucy gave Molly a sharp look. "Birth is a natural process. It's something our bodies are designed to do," she said, with a nod to the girls.

"Sadie says sometimes they cut the baby out," said Zoe, undermining Lucy's attempt to present childbirth in a positive light.

"That's true," said Molly. "It's called a caesarean."

"That must really hurt," said Deirdre.

"Not at all," said Lucy, climbing down with the jar of molasses. "They use anesthesia, like they do for any operation."

"And then they sew you up!" exclaimed Zoe, gleefully. "Sadie had stitches once, and she said it hurt real bad."

"Mummy says it's all worth it to have a beautiful baby like me," said Deirdre, dreamily. "She says I was such a beautiful baby, she was afraid the fairies would steal me."

Lucy set the molasses on the table with a thud. "Now, Deirdre, you know that's just make-believe. Fairies don't steal babies. Now, off you go."

"Thanks, Lucy," said Molly, picking up the jar and lumbering to her feet.

"Do you need anything else?"

"Nope, I've got it all. I'll bring some over when I've finished baking them."

"No, you won't," said Lucy, smiling.

"You're right," admitted Molly, buttoning her coat. "I'll probably eat them all, just like I ate a whole half gallon of coffee ice cream the other night." She grinned ruefully. "I can't seem to help myself. And the weird thing is, I never liked coffee ice cream before."

"It goes with the territory," said Lucy. "You're eating for two."

"Feels more like twenty sometimes," said Molly, closing the door behind her.

Lucy returned to her soup, chopping up carrots and celery and adding them to the pot. Moira hadn't said when she would pick Deirdre up, and Lucy wondered if she would still be with them at dinnertime. The Malones were an odd sort of family, she thought as she stirred the pot. Not exactly irresponsible parents, but awfully eager to assign child-care duties to someone else. And then there was the day they had discovered Old Dan's body, the very same day Dylan had come to the newspaper, seeking news of his brother. She remembered it clearly, how he'd come through the door, claiming he was right off the airplane, straight from Ireland that very day.

Maybe it was just a phrase, a bit of blarney, as Miss Tilley put it, or maybe Dylan Malone had indeed arrived in the country days ahead of his family. But why would he bother to lie about it? Perhaps he had a reason for keeping that information to himself.

Chapter Eight

After a bean soup supper on Sunday evening, Lucy took the script of *Finian's Rainbow* into the family room and settled down on the couch, joining Bill, who was in his usual spot, in the recliner, watching a *This Old House* rerun on PBS. She figured he must know every single show by heart, but he never tired of watching Tom Silva poking away at what seemed to be perfectly good siding and discovering rotted timbers underneath. The image of that crumbling wood—"Nothing holding this old house together except paint"—always gave her pause, since she knew that the last thing her highly regarded restoration carpenter husband wanted to do when he came home from a long day reconstructing somebody else's antique house was to work on his own antique house. She suspected the 150-year-old farmhouse was rotting away around them and occasionally had nightmares about the porch falling off, or about opening a door and stepping into a ruined room, with wallpaper hanging in shreds and gaps in the walls that you could see through. She didn't want to risk watching the show and discovering yet another potential problem, so she decided to ignore it and focus all her attention on the script.

Resolutely blocking words like *termite damage* and *rainwater seepage* from her consciousness, she was soon caught up in the story of Finian and his daughter, Sharon. She even found herself humming along to the songs.

"Lucy, that can't possibly be the tune," said Bill. "Are you sure they really want you in this show? Do they know you can't sing?"

"Frank Cahill, he's the musical director, was clearly underwhelmed by my talent," admitted Lucy. "But Moira insisted, and I'm in the chorus."

"Who's Moira?"

"She's married to the director, Dylan, and she's got the leading female role." Lucy paused. "She's also Deirdre's mother."

"Ah," said Bill. "It's all becoming clearer. She wants a baby-sitter for Deirdre."

"I think that might have something to do with it," said Lucy. "But I don't care. It's going to be fun, being in the show with Rachel and Pam." She didn't add the fact that her involvement with the Malones gave her an inside track on the murder, knowing that Bill would hardly approve of her conducting her own investigation.

Tom Silva and the crew had suddenly disappeared, and *This Old House* was replaced with a bank of phone operators and an ancient English actor pitching for donations to PBS. Bill flicked through the stations, looking for something else, and settled on a basketball game. "So what's the play about?"

"I've just started reading, but so far it's about an Irishman, Finian, who steals a pot of gold from a leprechaun and brings it to America so he can plant it near Fort Knox so it will grow and make him rich. He has the idea that all that government gold in Fort Knox will somehow fertilize his stash. He thinks all Americans are rich, that gold somehow grows here."

"That's news to me," said Bill. "Have you noticed any gold growing in our garden?"

"Not so far," said Lucy, "but I live in hope. This house

is so old, you'd think somebody sometime would have buried something valuable in the backyard. But all I ever find are bits of broken bottles and dishes. And bits of plastic toys, probably from our own kids."

"I know what you mean. Every time I rip out a wall in some old wreck, I'm hoping I'll find a sock full of gold coins that somebody stashed there and forgot, but all I ever seem to find are mouse nests."

"Old Dan was a bit of a miser," said Lucy, remembering how Dave Reilly had the same idea at the wake, when he tried to search the drawers and cabinets. "Maybe you'll find something at the Bilge."

"Believe me, I'm keeping my eyes peeled." He laughed. "Come to think of it, he was a bit like a leprechaun, wasn't he? Kinda little and stooped and wrinkled, and smoking that pipe of his. Maybe he did have a pot of gold stashed there."

Zoe padded into the room in her bare feet and pajamas, to kiss her parents good night before going to bed. "It's very difficult to take a leprechaun's gold," she said in a serious tone as she climbed onto her father's lap.

"And why is that?" he asked.

"They always come up with a trick," replied Zoe. "They make you look away or send you on an errand and promise to give it to you tomorrow. Something like that."

"But what if you trick the leprechaun?" Bill asked with a grin.

"It's very hard to trick a leprechaun. Almost impossible," said Zoe, with the conviction of a true believer. "But if you do, you can be sure the leprechaun will get you back. People in America think leprechauns are fat, jolly, happy little men, but Deirdre says that's wrong. They're really mean and spiteful, not jolly at all."

"You'd better think twice about taking that gold," Lucy told Bill. "If it does turn up, that is."

"Better leave it for the leprechaun," said Zoe. "And you know what else Deirdre told me?"

"Nope," replied Bill.

Zoe adopted a serious expression, as if about to impart some extremely valuable information. "Fairies aren't nice, either."

"Tinkerbell is nice," said Lucy.

"Not really," replied Zoe. "Remember how jealous she was of Wendy? Deirdre says that's typical. They're very vain and selfish little creatures."

"You're shattering all my illusions," complained Lucy. "Next thing you'll be telling me there's no Santa Claus."

"Mo-om," said Zoe, making the word two syllables and rolling her eyes for good measure. "You and Dad are Santa Claus. Nobody believes in Santa Claus."

"Okay, what about the tooth fairy? She's nice," said Lucy.

"You're the tooth fairy," said Zoe. "I know because you always forget and tell me to get back in bed and close my eyes, and then you tiptoe into my room." She furrowed her brow. "What do you do with all those teeth?"

"What teeth?" asked Lucy, all innocence.

"You know," said Zoe.

"Do not," insisted Lucy. "But I have heard that the tooth fairy gives them to other little children who don't have teeth yet. Only the good ones, of course. The ones without cavities or fillings."

"Fairies don't recycle teeth," said Zoe. "But they do steal little children."

"No, they don't," said Lucy. "Gypsies steal children. Everybody knows that."

"Fairies do, too," said Zoe. "Deirdre says so. They steal them and replace them with changelings."

"What's a changeling?" asked Bill.

"I'm not sure," admitted Zoe. "But I'm pretty sure they're no good."

"What do the fairies want with children, anyway?" asked Lucy. "Children are a lot more trouble than you

might think. You have to feed them and change their diapers, and sometimes they're fussy and they cry. It's hard to
imagine fairies being very good parents. They're too delicate and flighty. Not to mention that a human baby must
weigh a lot more than your average fairy. How do they
carry them?"

"I'm not sure," said Zoe, yawning. "I'll have to ask
Deirdre."

"You do that," said Lucy, giving her a hug. "And remember, all these creatures are make-believe. They're not
real. They're just stories. So you sleep tight and dream of
lollipops."

"I will, Mommy." She paused, holding her mother's
hand. "Will you tuck me in?"

Lucy looked at Bill. This was an unusual request. For
some time Zoe had insisted on putting herself to bed, insisting that only babies needed bedtime stories.

"Sure," said Lucy, getting up. "Would you like a story?
We haven't read *Make Way for Ducklings* in ages."

"Two stories," said Zoe, bargaining the way she used to
when she was younger and wanted to delay putting out
the light.

"Okay," said Lucy. "Two stories."

Lucy enjoyed cuddling with Zoe and rereading two of
her favorite children's books, *Make Way for Ducklings*
and *Blueberries for Sal*, lingering over the familiar words
and pictures in the well-worn copies, which had long ago
lost their dust jackets, but the reassuring bedtime ritual
didn't have the result she expected. Instead of sleeping like
a baby, Zoe spent a fitful night, disturbed by frightening
dreams. Lucy went to her bed twice, finding her shaking
and crying, and both times crawled into bed with her until
she fell asleep. Then she returned to her own bed, where
she herself tossed and turned, unable to sleep for worrying
about Zoe.

When Monday morning came, they were both tired. Lucy had two cups of coffee and made a mild coffee-milk for Zoe, in hopes of perking her up enough to get her off to school. The little dollop of coffee didn't have much effect, however, and it was a very sleepy little girl who dragged herself onto the school bus. Lucy was sure she'd get a call from the school nurse.

As it happened, the nurse didn't call, but the day seemed longer than usual, anyway. She didn't have enough energy to go out and track down those elusive prospectors for her feature story, so she worked on routine jobs, like the events listings, mortgage rates, property transfers, and the ever-popular police log listing all the DUI arrests in the past week. There were fewer DUIs than usual, which she figured was due to the fact that the Bilge was closed.

At lunchtime she headed over to Our Lady of Hope for a chorus rehearsal, but as she approached the church, she noticed a hearse parked outside, along with a black limousine and a handful of cars.

She assumed the rehearsal would be postponed. Frank, after all, would be needed to play the organ. But even if a substitute director could be found on such short notice, it would hardly be seemly to have the chorus singing jolly show tunes downstairs in the hall while a funeral was in progress upstairs in the sanctuary.

She went to the church hall, anyway, just to check, and found a notice announcing Old Dan's funeral on the door. Of course, she thought, the medical examiner had announced the autopsy results, which meant the body had been released to the family, who would want to bury it as soon as possible.

She followed the path around to the front of the church and was just in time to see the funeral director closing the door on the hearse. People were leaving the church and making their way to their cars for the procession to the cemetery. Lucy felt it would be rude to zoom off before the

procession was under way. People in Tinker's Cove took
funeral processions seriously: traffic came to a standstill,
and pedestrians stopped in their tracks on the sidewalk.
Men removed their hats as a sign of respect, and some
people even lowered their heads or crossed themselves
when one went by. So she waited in her car until the procession began moving, only to find herself waved into line
by one of the men from the funeral home. Might as well
go along, she decided. She really didn't have a choice, and
maybe she could write it up for the paper. Fortunately, because of the rehearsal, she had dressed more carefully than
usual and was wearing gray wool slacks instead of jeans
under her black winter parka. The duck boots were a mite
casual for a funeral, but she figured a lot of other people
would be wearing them.

When she arrived at the cemetery, she parked in line
with the other cars and made her way to the grave, where
the mourners had gathered. The snow cover was pretty
much gone, revealing soggy brown grass underfoot, but it
was cold, and the wind seemed to go right through her
parka. She shoved her hands in her pockets and tried not
to shiver as she joined the group.

Dylan was there, of course, hatless and wearing a
somber black topcoat. Moira cut her usual dramatic figure, with wildly blowing hair and the long black cape,
which was so voluminous that she had stood Deirdre in
front of her and wrapped it around her, too, leaving only
her little face exposed to the cruel weather.

A mere handful of Bilge regulars had showed up, including Frank Cahill. He was the best dressed of the group
in a wool suit and zippered down jacket. The rest were
wearing the working man's uniform of rubber boots, lined
jeans, and layers of shirts, sweaters, and thickly insulated
sweatshirts, which could be added or subtracted as
needed. Today the whole kit was required, and Lucy no-

ticed that a few had pulled their watch caps down over their ears and some had even pulled up their hoods over their hats.

Also in attendance were about a half dozen older women, bundled up in warm coats and layers of hats and scarves. She guessed they were regular churchgoers who never missed a funeral. A few were saying the rosary, whispering under their breath as they counted the beads with their gloved fingers.

There was a bit of chatter as people gathered, most avoiding looking at the yawning grave that awaited Old Dan's body and the mountain of earth beside it, covered with a green carpet of fake grass that looked extremely bright against the milky sky, bare trees, and brown grass. The conversation died, however, when Father Ed stepped forward and gave a nod, signaling the pallbearers to remove the casket from the hearse and carry it to the grave. She was watching this somber procedure when she noticed a late arrival: state police detective lieutenant Horowitz. He chose a spot on the opposite side from the mourners, standing beside the gravedigger. It seemed an odd choice to Lucy until she realized he had chosen that spot so he could see the faces of the mourners. That meant, she realized with a shiver, that he suspected the murderer was standing among them.

The graveside service was mercifully brief. Father Ed read the prescribed words for the burial ceremony from a small black book. They were slightly different from the familiar phrases in the Book of Common Prayer, which Lucy had heard so often, but expressed the same idea: we come into the world with nothing, and we leave it with nothing except the hope of eternal life in heaven. Then it was over, and people scattered, heading for the warmth of their cars. The gravedigger started up his backhoe, and Father Ed shook hands with Dylan and Moira and patted little Deirdre's head. Lucy made a beeline for Detective Horowitz.

"Have you got a minute?" she asked.

"I must have known you'd be here," he said, rubbing his nose with a gloved finger. "Otherwise, why would I have bothered to wear my long underwear? I must have known you'd have a zillion questions and would keep me standing out in the cold."

"Well I didn't wear my long underwear, so you won't get any sympathy from me," said Lucy, wrapping her arms across her chest and stamping her feet, which felt like frozen bricks. "And not a long list of questions, either." She paused. "I have some information that I think you might find useful."

"Ah," he said. "Nancy Drew has discovered a clue? In the grandfather clock, perhaps? Or the old mill?"

"I didn't know you were a fan," said Lucy.

"I have a niece," he said. He leveled his gaze at her and shook his head. "I only hope she doesn't turn out like you."

"I'm sure you're joking," said Lucy. "Do you want my information or not?"

He sighed. "Shoot."

"Well," she began, looking over her shoulder to make sure Dylan was out of earshot and discovering he was getting in the limousine, "I've learned that Dylan was in the country earlier than he said. He didn't come with his wife and daughter, but some time before them."

Horowitz drew his pale brows together, making a crease above his nose. "Are you sure?"

"His daughter told me he wasn't on the plane with her and Moira. He met them at the airport."

"Interesting," said Horowitz, raising an eyebrow.

"So you think he may be the killer?" asked Lucy.

"Could be," said Horowitz, keeping his face blank.

Lucy seized on this admission, hoping for a scoop. "Can I print that in the paper?"

"Sure," he said, with a slight smile. "You can say that at

this point we haven't eliminated anyone. Everyone's a suspect."

Lucy wasn't about to admit he'd dashed her hopes and came right back with a question. "So you haven't made much progress in the investigation?"

"Oh, I wouldn't say that," he said. Before she could follow up with another question, he continued. "And, by the way, a piece of advice. Leave this investigation to us. This killer is a very dangerous person and I . . . well, I was going to say I'd hate to see you get hurt, but the truth is, you're a nuisance, and my job would be a lot simpler without you poking your nose in where it doesn't belong, but I'm sure your husband and children would miss you. So keep that in mind, okay?"

For once, Lucy was speechless and stood mute, jaw dropped in astonishment, as Horowitz marched off toward his unmarked car. "And I thought he liked me," she muttered as she, too, hurried to get out of the wind and into the shelter of her Subaru.

But no sooner had she seated herself behind the wheel and started the engine than she noticed the prospector Paul Sullivan walking slowly among the gravestones and scanning the ground with his metal detector. Realizing that she couldn't pass up this serendipitous opportunity to continue her interview, she reluctantly got out of the car, leaving the engine running and the heater on high.

"I say, you must be cold," she said, hailing him. "Do you want to sit for a bit in my car and get warm?"

"No thanks," he said. "I dress for the weather." It was true. His entire body was encased in a bright orange jumpsuit. "This is official Coast Guard winter gear. I got it from a guy who was retiring. It's what the Coasties wear out at sea. It's the best you can get."

"I could use one," said Lucy, resolving to make this interview short. "So tell me. Do you find a lot of valuables in the cemetery?" For a moment an awful thought crossed her mind. He couldn't possibly be digging up jewelry from the graves, could he?

As if reading her mind, he answered, "The dead don't give up anything, but the living do." He showed her the small change he'd collected, along with a gold ring. "It's not from a grave. Couldn't be, because the dead are all buried in coffins. Somebody must've dropped it."

"Nonetheless," she said, with a shudder, "some people might think there's something kind of creepy about prospecting in the cemetery."

"Some people are afraid of ghosts," he said, with a wink. "But not me. I like it here. It's quiet, and it reminds me of something my mother used to say when somebody crossed her."

"What was that?" asked Lucy.

"It's an old Irish curse," he said, chuckling and sweeping his metal detector across the dead grass. "May the grass grow before your door."

Lucy was back in the car, holding her frozen hands in front of the heat vents, before she realized what it meant. If the grass was growing unchecked on the path to your front door, it meant you weren't coming and going. You no longer walked the earth, because you were dead.

Chapter Nine

Saturday morning a light, wet snow was falling but wasn't enough to get excited about. Moira, however, didn't see it that way when she arrived bright and early to drop off Deirdre. Sara had been pressed into service as a rather unwilling child minder while Lucy was at the rehearsal. "Not a baby-sitter, Mo-om," insisted Zoe, "because we're not babies."

"Oh yes, you are," said Sara. "If you need a baby-sitter, you're a baby."

"Am not."

"Are so."

And so it went until Lucy came up with the politically correct term of *child minder* and sweetened the deal by promising to pay Sara a couple of dollars an hour, far below the going rate but better than nothing at all. Nevertheless, Sara was hardly civil when Moira and Deirdre arrived. Moira couldn't get over the snow and exclaimed about it while Lucy removed Deirdre's parka.

"We don't get much snow in Ireland, you know. I wish we did. It's *so* beautiful. I *love* the way it sticks to the trees and turns everything *ordinary* into a *winter wonderland*. It's like *fairyland*, isn't it, Deirdre?"

Melting snowflakes glistened in Deirdre's jet-black hair and stuck to her long eyelashes, making the little girl look even more beautiful and ethereal than usual. "Can we play in the snow?" she asked.

"Sure," said Lucy, "if it's all right with Sara. She's in charge while your mother and I are at the rehearsal."

"And I don't want any nonsense from you midgets, either," said Sara, pouring milk into her bowl of cereal.

"Sara, you need to adjust your attitude," chided Lucy. "I'm counting on you to be responsible and to set a good example."

"Sure, Mom," said Sara, shuffling off to the family room in her fuzzy slippers.

"It's just an act," an embarrassed Lucy told Moira. "She's really very reliable. She'll take good care of the girls."

"I don't doubt it. I remember being a rebellious teenager myself. I must have driven my mum to distraction. I was crazy about the boys," said Moira as they left the house and got in her car. "I used to sneak out of my room at night and go off to the clubs with my girlfriends. We were underage, but they always let us in. We'd dance all night and then be too tired to get up for school the next morning. We'd have to go, though, and the sisters would be furious with us when we couldn't keep our eyes open in class."

She started the car and reversed neatly enough, but when she shifted into drive and pressed the gas pedal, the car skidded crosswise down the drive, fortunately coming to a stop before the mailbox.

"What happened?" asked Moira, wide-eyed.

"You're not used to driving in snow," said Lucy, trying to seem calm even though her heart was pounding. "You need to go slow and accelerate very gently, and if you start to skid, steer into the skid and, whatever you do, don't brake."

"But how do I stop the car if I can't brake?"

"You go slow to start with, and you anticipate stops,

tapping the brake gently so you don't lose control." Lucy
paused, letting her advice sink in. "Are you ready?"

"Ready as I'll ever be," said Moira, backing the car
slowly away from the mailbox and then creeping onto Red
Top Road, fishtailing slightly as she made the turn. "I'm
beginning to think snow isn't quite as wonderful as I
thought," she said. "Maybe rainy old Ireland isn't so bad
after all."

They were late arriving at the church hall, and the rehearsal was in full swing. Brian Donahue and the crew
were hard at work at the rear of the stage, hammering the
scenery together. Frank was at the piano, leading the chorus in some warm-up vocalization exercises, and Dylan
was coaching Dave Reilly, who was playing the lead part
of Woody, on his lines. No wonder he was having trouble,
thought Lucy as she hurried over to take her place with the
chorus. The Claws' rock repertoire was bigger on wails
and groans than actual lyrics.

Now that she had a couple of chorus rehearsals under
her belt, Lucy felt a lot more comfortable singing with the
group and thought she did all right. She didn't get any
dirty looks from the others, and Frank didn't single her
out for a correction as he did some of the singers. They'd
gone through all of the songs and been instructed to know
the lyrics by heart for the next rehearsal when Frank in-
troduced Tatiana Olsen, the local dance teacher who was
playing the part of Susan.

Lucy knew Tatiana from the days when Elizabeth and
Sara took ballet lessons, but she hadn't seen her in a while.
Amazingly enough, she didn't seem to have aged a bit. Her
long hair was still dark and glossy, her back was straight,
and she hadn't gained a pound.

"Look at her," whispered Pam, with a nudge. "Doesn't
she look fabulous?"

"It must be all that dancing," whispered Rachel.

"Exercise really works," said Lucy, with a huge sigh. "It's not fair."

"Tatiana's going to teach you some basic dance steps," Frank told the chorus members, then called for Moira to join them. "We need you, Moira, for the first act finale, and you, too, Woody, I mean, Dave."

With a nod to Dylan, Dave bounded up onto the stage and made a low, sweeping bow to Tatiana, as if he were D'Artagnan bowing before the Queen of France. The flamboyant gesture wasn't missed by Moira, who was across the room, pouring herself a cup of coffee. Narrowing her eyes, she took her time, adding sugar and creamer and leaving the paper packets scattered on the table, completely ignoring the trash basket.

"Moira, darling, we're waiting," called Frank, and all heads turned in her direction. Only then, when she was certain everyone was watching, did she begin her approach to the stage, sipping her coffee as she crossed the room. Finally reaching the steps to the stage, she set her half-empty cup on a windowsill, then took her place next to Dave.

Frank looked about ready to explode, his face and even his ears turning an unhealthy shade of red, but Tatiana remained serene, arranging the chorus members behind the leading couple and teaching them all some simple combinations to accompany "Great Come-And-Get-It Day," the rousing song and dance number that climaxed the first act. After running through the steps a few times, she suggested they try it with the music. Frank took his place at the piano, and they stumbled through the number, trying to dance and read their sheet music at the same time. Tatiana, meanwhile, instructed Moira and Dave in their solo *pas de deux*, performed in front of the swaying and humming group while singing a few lines as a duet.

Moira had no trouble at all projecting her, or rather

Sharon's, interest in Woody by swinging her hips provocatively and holding hands rather longer than necessary, but when she attempted to sing her line, she was only able to gasp out a few words before giving up entirely.

Frank abruptly banged out a chord, bringing everything to a sudden stop. "Moira, my dear," he began, speaking in an extremely condescending tone, "this simply won't do. It needs to be lively, darling. It should trip off your tongue while your little feet are doing their thing. We'll have to think of something." He adopted a thoughtful pose, scratching his chin, and then lifted his face as if suddenly inspired. "I know. We'll record your part, and you can lip-synch. How's that?"

Moira glared at him. "Who do you think I am? Ashlee Simpson?"

"Now, now, darling. You know they all do it. All the big stars do it in concert," said Frank. "You don't think million-dollar divas can do all those gymnastics and then belt out a tune. It can't be done. There's no shame in it." He paused. "We have the technology."

"Technology be damned," she said. "What if it doesn't work? Then I'm stuck out there looking a fool. I won't do it."

"Well, what do you suggest, then?" asked Frank.

"For one thing," she began, tossing her head and glaring at Tatiana, "we could adjust the choreography. I know your intentions are good, but you're obviously an *amateur*. This number calls for an entirely different approach. It needs to be reworked. It's simply no good." She smiled condescendingly at Tatiana. "Trust me. I know what pleases an audience."

Tatiana lifted her chin and stared at Moira through her lashes. "I'll see what I can do," she said. "I tend to forget that most people aren't in dancing shape."

Moira pulled herself up to her full height and was about to deliver a retort but was cut off by Frank.

"The choreography's not the problem," he declared, smiling at Tatiana, "and we don't have time to change it. The show's in four weeks." He sat back down at the piano and played a few notes before turning to Moira. "I would have thought a *professional* like yourself would have come better prepared."

"How dare you!" shrieked Moira, with a dramatic toss of her head. "Who do you think you are—a church organist, for Chrissake—to criticize me, who's been appearing on stage ever since I was six years old!"

Frank turned to Tatiana. "And she still acts like she's six years old."

"That's it!" declared Moira, stamping her feet. "I'm not sticking around to be insulted! I'm out of here!"

And they all watched openmouthed as she grabbed her cloak from the chair it was lying on and stormed out of the hall, slamming the door behind her so hard that her half-empty cup of coffee toppled off the windowsill and splashed on the floor.

"Oh, dear," said Lucy, nudging Rachel and Pam, "there goes my ride."

Dylan watched her go, then approached Frank. Unlike his temperamental wife, Dylan seemed calm and collected, with a businesslike expression on his face.

Frank struck a chord on the piano. "Take ten, people," he said.

The cast members broke into little groups. Some helped themselves to coffee from the industrial-size pot on the counter that divided the hall from the kitchen, a few went outside for a smoke, and others got Cokes from the machine in the hall. Rachel cleaned up the spilled coffee, then joined Pam and Lucy on the row of seats set along the wall.

"Only four weeks 'til Saint Patrick's Day," said Rachel. "Do you think we'll be ready?"

"Not if the star of the show walks out whenever things don't go her way," said Lucy.

"Come on," said Pam. "Frank was awfully hard on her. Nobody knows their lines yet."

"I don't agree," said Rachel. "He was right. A professional should have prepared, gotten her voice in shape, and learned the songs, taken some dancing classes."

"Maybe you'll get the part after all," said Lucy, nudging Rachel. "Frank seems pretty ticked off."

Frank's face had gotten quite red, and he was apparently mincing no words in his discussion with Dylan, even though he was keeping his voice low. Whatever he was saying, Dylan didn't seem to be taking it well. Finally, he erupted and shouted, "You may be the musical director, but don't forget, I'm the director. I"—he was stabbing his chest—"make the final decisions!"

Frank stood a moment, glaring at him, then capitulated. "Okay, but it's your funeral," he said, sitting back down on the bench.

"My funeral if she loses the part," muttered Dylan, pulling a pack of cigarettes from his jacket pocket and heading outside.

Lucy and her friends overheard him as he marched past, and they had a good laugh together.

"I think I'll call home and see how Sara's making out," said Lucy, pulling out her cell phone. She couldn't get a clear signal, so she began walking around the room, even trying the stage, where she found Brian on his hands and knees, hammering studs together.

"Forget it," he said. "This building's in a dead zone or something. You might have better luck outside."

Lucy looked out the window, where the snow was falling thicker than ever. "I guess I'll pass," she said, pocketing the phone. "How's the scenery coming?"

He rolled his eyes. "Dylan there thinks we can whip up

Irish countryside and rural Missitucky, complete with a babbling brook and bridge, in four weeks and with a budget of five hundred bucks." He shrugged. "You know the price of wood. It can't be done."

"No, it can't," she agreed. "Has he got the same attitude about the Bilge renovations?"

"I gotta hand it to your husband," said Brian, with an admiring nod. "He's got a way with him. He's got Dylan thinking it's a privilege to write checks to him."

"Well," said Lucy, "he is a fine craftsman."

"That he is. I'm learning a lot from him." He sat back on his heels. "Looks like Frank isn't getting along any better with Dylan than he did with his brother," he said.

This was news to Lucy. "Frank didn't like Old Dan?" she asked.

"They had their moments," he said, chuckling. "They had a big fight one night, and Old Dan kicked him out."

"Not an unusual occurrence at the Bilge," said Lucy. "At least not from what I've heard."

He shrugged. "Yeah, there was usually some sort of fight most nights—but not with Old Dan. He was off-limits. But not to Frank. He hauled off and socked him, gave the old guy a black eye."

"What was it about?" asked Lucy.

"To tell the truth, I'm not sure. Frank gets a bit touchy when he drinks too much."

"Touchy enough to kill Old Dan?"

Brian's eyebrows shot up. "Frank? Kill somebody? No way."

Lucy wasn't quite so willing to dismiss Frank as a suspect. He had a mean streak; she'd seen it in the way he taunted Moira. And after years as a reporter covering local tragedies, she believed that almost anyone, given the right circumstances, could resort to violence. Battered wives finally turned on their abusive husbands, husbands with financial problems or a mistress killed the wife and kids rather than confess, old folks who could no longer manage their senile spouses found a drug overdose or a pillow could provide a quick solution, and old feuds that had simmered for years sometimes boiled over into fisticuffs or worse. She was thinking along these lines when she was interrupted by another piano chord.

"Okay, girls and boys, it's time to get back to work," announced Frank. "There's plenty we can do while our leading lady gets over her hissy fit." He flipped through the score. "I know. Let's do 'The Begat.' That's a nice rousing number. Chorus! Senator Rawkins! Places, please."

"The Begat" was indeed a rousing number, and Lucy was humming it when Rachel dropped her off at home a couple of hours later. An inch or two of wet snow had fallen, and the roads hadn't been cleared yet, making the going rather tricky even for an experienced Maine driver like Rachel. Lucy hoped Moira's first stop after leaving the rehearsal was to fetch Deirdre and take her home. She didn't like to think of Moira attempting it now on the slippery roads.

But when she went into the house, stamping the snow off her boots and calling out that she was home, there was no answer. The house had that quiet, empty feeling that meant no one was home, not even the dog.

A couple of empty mugs with the dregs of hot chocolate in the bottom sat on the kitchen table, an encouraging sign that Sara had taken her child-minding responsibilities seriously. Lucy assumed she had taken everyone out for a walk in the snow and sat down on the bench by the kitchen door to unlace her boots. She hadn't really expected Sara to do anything so ambitious, but perhaps she'd got tired of being cooped up in the house all morning with the younger girls. Or perhaps Deirdre had begged to go out in the snow, which was a novelty to her. Or maybe Bill had come home from work early and taken them all sliding, as he sometimes did. Whatever the reason for this blissful peace, she decided she was going to take advantage of it and stretch out on the couch with a book. She only got through a few pages, however, before she dozed off and the book dropped to the floor.

It was there that Sara, and Libby, found her about twenty minutes later.

"Mom! Wake up!"

Sara was shaking her shoulder, and Libby was licking her face. "Whuh?" was all she could manage to say.

Sara was leaning over her. "Did Deirdre's mom come? Did she take Zoe, too?"

"What do you mean?" asked Lucy, suddenly alert.

"The girls were here when I left. I only went out for a minute to put the dog in her run, but she slipped out and she ran off before I could catch her. I was afraid she'd get lost in the snow, so I followed her, and it took longer than I thought. But when I left, the girls were sitting at the table, drinking hot chocolate."

"I dunno," said Lucy. "They weren't here when I got home. Maybe Moira came while you were gone."

"I don't think so, Mom," said Sara. "I wasn't that far from the house. I heard your car, but that's all."

"I'm pretty sure I saw tire tracks in the driveway," said Lucy, standing up.

"Not anymore. It's stopped snowing," said Sara, pointing toward the window. "It's been raining for at least fifteen minutes."

It was true. The snow was melting fast, falling off the trees in great wet plops of slush, and the driveway was a soupy sea of slush. Remembering Moira's frame of mind when she left the rehearsal, Lucy considered the possibility that she might have gone off on her own, deciding to take some time to soothe her ruffled spirits. "If Moira didn't pick them up, what do you think happened? Do you think they went out on their own?"

Sara bit her lip. "I don't think so, Mom. I gave them strict orders not to, and besides, they'd been playing outside earlier, and their coats and mittens and snow pants were soaking wet. I put them in the dryer, and it was still running when I went after the dog."

Lucy hurried through the dining room and kitchen, into the laundry room, and yanked open the dryer door. There was nothing there except a crumpled sheet of fabric softener. Lucy picked it up and fingered it, trying not to panic. "They're gone," she said, struggling to control the fear—and guilt—that threatened to overwhelm her. "We have to find them."

Chapter Ten

Lucy's hands shook as she zipped her parka and pulled the hood over her head. She tried to calm herself, tried to believe she was overreacting, but one look at Sara's white face and enormous, fear-filled eyes sent her dashing for the door. Sara handed her the dog's leash, and Libby sprang out through the barely open door, pulling her right across the porch and sending her flying down the stairs. All of a sudden she was flat on the ground, her hands and face in the cold, wet muck. Her knees and elbows hurt, but she ignored them, scrambling to her feet and hanging on to the leash as Libby dragged her through the slippery mush.

"Zoe! Deirdre! Zoe!" yelled Lucy, but there was no answer from the glistening black trunks of the fir trees, no reply from the slick, lichen-covered boulders or the blank white sky. The sleety rain continued to fall, soaking through her "guaranteed waterproof" parka, but she didn't feel it as she sloshed through the icy mess, desperately searching for any footprints, any sign of the girls.

It was all this nonsense about fairies and the snow transforming the woods into fairyland, she thought as the dog dragged her deeper into the woods, slipping and sliding with every step. But why hadn't they come back to the house when it started to rain? Had they found some sort of shelter? A hut built by kids, maybe, or a tarp erected by one of the homeless wanderers who occasionally took up residence by the pond? Or had they had some sort of accident?

Perhaps they had slipped and fallen, breaking bones. Or a heavy branch had broken off a tree and pinned them to the ground. But even Lucy, deranged with worry as she was, had to admit it was unlikely that they both would have been hurt, and she couldn't understand why the unhurt girl wouldn't have come back to the house for help. And lurking in the back of her mind was the resentful conviction that whatever had happened, it was probably Deirdre's doing. That child was too flighty, too caught up in make-believe, and she never should have let Zoe spend so much time with her.

Lucy checked her pocket for her cell phone and made sure it was working so Sara, who was back at the house, could call if they showed up there. It was fully charged but remained stubbornly silent, so she plowed on to Blueberry Pond, a frequent scene of winter tragedy as eager skaters often ventured out onto ice that was too thin to support them, or snowmobilers dared each other to race across and didn't make it. But there was no sign of the girls at the pond, where the frozen surface was smooth and unbroken beneath a thin, translucent layer of rainwater.

No sign of the girls anywhere. Standing there under the white sky in the bleak, empty landscape, Lucy was beginning to think the unthinkable: that they had been abducted.

Squeezing the cell phone tight with her wet gloved hand, she checked in with Sara at the house. "Maybe they went to Toby's?" suggested Sara.

"Of course," exclaimed Lucy, seizing on the idea. Zoe adored Toby and Molly's little house on Prudence Path. The girls might have sought shelter there; they might have just gone for a visit.

But when Molly opened the door, with a puzzled expression on her face, Lucy knew they weren't there.

"What's the matter?" asked Molly, seeing her worried face and taking in her soaking wet clothes and the exhausted, panting dog.

"Zoe and her friend Deirdre are missing," said Lucy. "Have you seen them?"

Molly shook her head. "Are you sure they're not in the house? Why would they be out in this weather?"

"We think they might be hunting for fairies," said Lucy. "Deirdre's obsessive about fairies, and she thinks they like snow. I'm afraid they went out and got lost or had some sort of accident."

Molly's eyes widened, and her hand went to her bulging tummy. "The pond!"

"I checked."

Molly let out a sigh of relief. "Lucy, you're soaking wet. Come in and call the neighbors. They might've gone to one of them."

She tried to coax Lucy out of her wet clothes, but Lucy refused, saying she couldn't give up the search. Molly settled for toweling off Libby and giving her a bowl of water while Lucy called the neighbors. There were four other houses on Prudence Path, but only Renee LaChance and Willie Westwood were home. Neither one had seen the girls. "Not hide nor hair," said Willie, whose husband was a vet. "Call me if you need help searching," she added. "I can cover a lot of ground on horseback."

"I hope it won't come to that," said Lucy, resigned to returning home without the girls. As she slipped and slid along the slushy path to home, hanging on to the dog with one hand and holding the other out for balance, she almost managed to convince herself that she had somehow missed the girls in her frantic search of the house. Maybe they'd gone down to the cellar or up to the attic; maybe they were playing hide-and-seek. But as soon as she stepped back into the silent house, she knew it was a delusion. She slipped off her soaking parka, and she and Sara and Libby searched, anyway, even using flashlights to peer under beds and into closets, just to make sure. But Lucy knew in her heart that they weren't there.

She was just about to pick up the phone to call Bill when there was a loud knocking at the door. She ran to answer, her heart pounding, certain it was the girls. Her hopes plummeted when she realized it was Dylan.

"Good day to you," he said in his hearty Irish brogue. "My good wife left me a note instructing me to pick up our wee colleen here at exactly half past one." He tapped his wristwatch and winked. "And as you can see, I am exactly on time."

Lucy didn't know how to begin. How do you tell a father that you've accidentally mislaid his child?

"I see from your expression that there's some problem," he said, stepping inside and removing his tweed cap. "Is it that I got the time wrong?"

Lucy shook her head, still mute.

"Well, what is it then, woman? The house seems mighty quiet, considering my Deirdre always causes a bit of commotion."

"They're not here." Lucy finally got the words out.

"Well, where are they, then?"

"I don't know."

Dylan's fleshy face flushed red. "YOU DON'T KNOW?" he thundered. "WHY NOT?"

Lucy jumped, startled by his yelling, and tried to explain with a trembling voice. "My older daughter Sara was minding them so I could go to the rehearsal. Moira knew, of course, and it was fine with her. But at some point in the afternoon, the dog got out and Sara gave chase, and when she got back to the house, the girls were missing. We've looked all over, but there's no sign of them."

"That's right," said Sara, who had heard Dylan's bellow and came to explain. "They were sitting right there at the table, having some hot chocolate, when I left. I only thought I'd be gone for a minute, but the dog ran over to my brother's house—they give her treats—and when I got back, the girls were gone."

"I think your wife must have picked them up," suggested Lucy.

"But why would she leave me instructions to do it?" asked Dylan. "You were there, so you know how upset she was at the rehearsal, all due to that unprofessional ignoramus. She left a note saying she was going to go for a walk to cool off and would I please pick up Deirdre."

"And even if she changed her mind, why would she take Zoe, too?" asked Lucy. "It doesn't make sense."

"What doesn't make sense is why you would leave two little girls in the care of an unreliable teenager," said Dylan, glaring at Sara.

"Sara's not unreliable," said Lucy. "She gave up her Saturday morning to watch the girls."

"She was probably on the phone with her boyfriend the whole time," said Dylan. "I bet she wouldn't have noticed if they'd set the house on fire."

"That's not true," said Sara. "I took them outside and played with them in the snow. I made hot chocolate for them. . . ."

"I don't believe a word of it. I'm sure you just watched TV," replied Dylan.

"Just a minute," protested Lucy. "If Sara said she played with them and gave them hot chocolate, well then, she did. She tells the truth, unlike some people."

His bristly brows shot together. "And what's that supposed to mean? Are you calling me a liar?"

Lucy didn't like being on the spot like this, but she didn't see any way out except to go forward. "You know what I mean. You're a bit loose with the truth yourself, now aren't you?"

"What exactly do you mean?" he demanded, glaring at her.

Lucy swallowed hard. "Well, for example, you didn't exactly come on the plane with your family like you said you did."

"What's that got to do with anything?" said Dylan, dismissing her accusation. "Lots of husbands and wives take separate planes in case of a crash. What I want to know is what you've done with my daughter."

"I have done nothing except give your daughter a playmate. If anything, I think it's your daughter who's caused the problem here," said Lucy. "My Zoe is a sensible child, at least she was until she started playing with your Deirdre. Now she can't sleep for fear of demons and leprechauns and I don't know what all."

"Now that's not fair," protested Dylan. "Deirdre has a healthy imagination and enjoys a bit of make-believe, but she's not a naughty child."

"I don't know what you consider healthy—"

"Mom," interrupted Sara. "Whatever's going on here, there's no sense looking for someone to blame. We need to find the girls, and arguing isn't helping."

Ashamed, Lucy bit her lip. "I'm going to call my husband," she told Dylan.

He nodded in agreement.

Bill didn't mince any words when she told him what had happened. "Call the police," he said. "I'm on my way home."

"The police? Are you sure?" replied Lucy. "What if they're just hiding or it's some silly misunderstanding. . . ?"

"Don't be ridiculous," said Bill. "This is what police are for. Call them, or I will."

"I'll do it," she said.

She started dialing the number, which she knew by heart because she'd called it so many times as a reporter, but Dylan grabbed the phone from her and punched in 911.

"Yes, we have an emergency," he said. "Two missing children."

It was then that Lucy felt tears pricking her eyes, and she quickly brushed them away. Until now she'd been just barely able to control her emotions by refusing to believe the girls were really missing. She'd clung to the notion that there was some misunderstanding, some mistake. But that was shattered when she heard Dylan's call for help. This was the real thing, a real emergency. Two little girls were gone.

Lucy's friend Officer Barney Culpepper answered the call, arriving at the same time as Bill. From the window, Lucy watched as they shook hands in the yard, then came into the house together. Bill took her in his arms while Barney stood aside, gripping his cap in his hand.

"I'm going to need some information," said Barney. "The sooner I get it, the sooner we can find those girls."

"Right," said Lucy. The tears had started to flow again, and she wiped them away with the back of her hand.

"Mebbe it would be best if we all sat down at the table," said Barney. "I don't know about you, but I could sure use some coffee."

"I'll make it," said Lucy. "Sara was minding them. She can tell you what happened."

She filled the pot with water and counted out the scoops of coffee, with shaking hands, listening as Sara recounted the story. By the time she finished and flicked the switch, she felt much calmer. When she joined the others at the table, Barney had turned to Dylan.

"So you came to pick up your daughter at one thirty?"

"That's right."

"What about your wife?" asked Barney.

"What about her?"

"How come she didn't pick up the little girl? Isn't that the more usual arrangement?"

"Actually, she was supposed to pick them up, but she left a note asking me to do it instead."

"And why was that?"

"She was upset. We'd been rehearsing the show at the church, and she had a disagreement with the musical director."

"She left the rehearsal early?"

"Yes."

"And would you say she was angry or upset?"

"I don't think . . ."

"I do," said Lucy. "She was definitely upset when she left."

"So it's possible she picked up the girls herself?" asked Barney.

"It's possible, but not probable," insisted Dylan. "I know my wife, and I'm sure she would have let me know if she decided to change plans, and the last I knew, she wanted some time to herself."

Barney scratched his chin. "What kind of car does she drive?"

"A little white compact. It's a rental," said Dylan.

"Ah, good. I'll contact the rental company and get the license number. It's possible we can put out an AMBER Alert," said Barney.

Despite Lucy's best efforts to control herself, a sob escaped, and Bill took her hand.

"What is this AMBER Alert?" demanded Dylan.

"We'll issue a description of your wife and the girls and the car. It will go out to all police units in Maine as well as the neighboring states, and on TV and radio, too. It works real good. We often get a sighting within minutes."

"But you're turning my wife into a criminal. Anyone

who hears this AMBER Alert will think she's a kidnapper," protested Dylan.

"She's the best lead we've got," said Barney. "She's missing, too. She was in an emotional state. Chances are, she took the girls." He licked his pencil. "Now can you give me some descriptions?"

When Dylan remained silent, glumly staring at the table, Lucy spoke up. "Moira has red hair, one hundred twenty pounds, five foot six, something like that, wears a black cape. Deirdre is eight or nine years old, with dark hair and green eyes, wearing a pink parka. Zoe is ten, with light brown hair, and is wearing a blue jacket and snow pants."

"Good. I'll radio it in," said Barney.

The cackle of his radio filled the kitchen as he filed his report. Then, finishing, he turned to Lucy and patted her hand. "Don't worry. We'll find them."

It was then Lucy remembered the coffee. She got up to get cups and pour it out when there was a knock on the door, and Toby came in, along with Willie, Renee, and her mother, Frankie, all from Prudence Path. They were all dressed for the weather, Willie in tall boots and a long raincoat with split seams for riding.

"Any news?" asked Toby.

"Not yet," said Barney. "It's just a matter of time."

"Right." Toby nodded. "Well, we thought we might take a look around outside, check the backyards and woods. Is there any objection?"

"Mom already did that," said Sara.

"Won't hurt to do it again," said Barney.

"I'll go, too," said Dylan, standing up.

"I'm going to the stable to get my horse," said Willie, giving Lucy a little smile. "Blaze and I can cover a lot of ground. If they're out there, we'll find them."

They all clattered out, leaving the kitchen suddenly

quiet, with only Bill and Barney sitting at the table, nursing their coffee. Lucy went into the powder room to wash her face.

The reflection she saw in the mirror shocked her. Her eyes were red and swollen, her face blotchy, and when she put the cool washcloth against her burning eyes, it only made the tears start to flow again. She put the toilet lid down and sat on it, taking deep breaths and telling herself that everything would be all right. When no more tears would come, she ran the cold water, gave her face a final wipe, and went back to join Bill and Barney in the kitchen.

Their backs were to her, and they didn't notice her return but continued their conversation as she went to the counter to pour herself a cup of coffee. She had just picked up the pot when she heard Barney say, "You might think I'm jumping the gun here, but there's no time to waste. The truth is, three-quarters of abducted children who are murdered are dead within three hours of the abduction."

Chapter Eleven

The carafe dropped from her hands and rolled across the floor, leaving a trail of dark brown coffee. Lucy stood, staring at the mess, terrified by the possibility that Zoe might be gone forever. Until then, she had only given a passing thought to the possibility that the girls might have been abducted. She hadn't seriously considered the fact that they could have been snatched by some weird pervert, but she knew it happened. The news was always reporting these tragic stories of abuse and death. Babies ripped from their mothers' bodies, children snatched out of bed or off the sidewalk and hidden away, forced to gratify their captors' twisted desires. And then . . .

"It's going to be all right," said Bill, taking her in his arms.

"Now, now," said Barney, reaching for a towel and dropping to his knees to mop up the mess. "What you heard, that's just part of the story. The truth is that most missing children are found safe and sound. Only a very small minority are actually victims of"—he paused and humpfed— "predators."

"But it's a possibility," said Lucy. "You read about it in the papers all the time. Amber and Jessica and Jeffrey and Megan. I don't want Zoe on that list."

"That's the trouble," said Barney, lumbering clumsily to

his feet and putting the coffee-soaked towel in the sink. The carafe, miraculously unbroken, he set back in place on the coffeemaker, which he switched off. "These sensational cases get all the publicity. You never hear about the kid who went to play at his friend's house and forgot to call home. Or the mom who takes her child's friend along for a ride to the candy store and loses track of time."

"Do you think that's what happened?" asked Lucy.

"I'm sure it is," said Barney, looking anxiously at the clock.

Lucy knew what he was thinking. It was after two, which meant less than three hours of daylight left, maybe less on this gloomy day. The roar of an engine caught her attention, and she looked out the window, spotting two more neighbors, Preston and Tommy Stanton, joining the search on ATVs. She also saw the sky had darkened, filled with threatening black clouds. She went into the family room, where she found Molly was keeping Sara company. Libby was stretched out at their feet, on the carpeted floor.

"Any news?" Sara asked eagerly.

Lucy shook her head.

"Mom, it wasn't my fault, really," said Sara. "They're not babies. It was all right to leave them, wasn't it? I was so scared the dog would get hit by a car or something."

It wasn't an unreasonable fear. Libby's predecessor, Kudo, had been hit by a truck and killed on Red Top Road. Lucy sat on the couch, beside Sara, and wrapped her arm around her shoulder, pulling her close. "I would have done the same thing," she said. Libby had gotten up and was resting her chin on Lucy's knee, and Lucy scratched her behind her ears. "Libby's part of the family, too. Besides, Zoe ought to know better than to go off without permission."

"That's what scares me," admitted Sara. "I'm afraid she was forced to go, against her will."

Lucy squeezed her daughter tighter. Molly sat quietly, rubbing her stomach.

"That Deirdre struck me as a pretty spooky kid," said Molly. "Remember how she told me that I should watch out for fairies after I have the baby, because fairies like to steal babies?" Molly paused. "The weird part is that she really seemed to believe it. It wasn't like she was telling some silly old story or anything. She was dead serious."

"It was all she talked about," agreed Sara. "I tried to get her interested in some other game, like Monopoly, or watching a video, but all she wanted to do was play fairies."

"It's probably just a phase," said Lucy. "Kids have these fads. Toby was mad about dinosaurs. Elizabeth absolutely had to have a kitten. I guess fairies are less trouble than a kitten."

"Not according to Deirdre," said Sara. "Fairies are nothing but trouble. Though I can't see why they want to steal babies. It's not as if a fairy would make a very good mother."

"It's just a myth, a way of explaining birth defects," said Molly. "People didn't understand why a baby was colicky or slow to develop, so they blamed it on the fairies. The fairies stole the healthy baby and left a sickly one in its place. A changeling."

Lucy remembered how she had worried during her own pregnancies for fear her baby wouldn't be healthy. She glanced at Molly, wondering if she had the same fears, and noticed that she looked different somehow. She'd lost that pregnant glow, she realized. Her face was puffier than before, and her blond hair had lost its former shine. She reached out and patted her knee. "Well, if there's one thing I'm certain of, it's that fairies did not abduct Zoe and Deirdre," said Lucy.

She got up and went out to the kitchen, where Bill and Barney were still sitting at the table. Seeing her, Barney shook his head. "No news," he said.

Lucy looked at the clock. A quarter hour had passed since she last checked the time. Fifteen minutes. Not long.

But how many minutes had Zoe been gone? Sixty, seventy, ninety, maybe more. She could already be ninety miles from home.

"So what exactly went out on this AMBER Alert?" she asked.

"The girls' descriptions, and Moira's, too, and a description of her car and license number, on the chance that they might be with her," said Barney.

"You'd think someone would have spotted them by now," said Bill. "Especially since it's been on the radio."

"And Moira's pretty noticeable, with her red hair and that black cape," said Lucy.

"A hat and a different coat and she would no longer match the description," said Barney.

Lucy felt a new emptiness in her gut, realizing it was possible that Moira herself had abducted the girls. "We don't really know the Malones, do we? We don't know that they really are who they say they are. We all just took Dylan and Moira at face value, believing everything they said."

"We had no reason not to," said Bill. "Besides, people are trusting. It's human nature. Almost anyone can be conned."

"These con men are good actors," said Barney. "Some of them even believe their own nonsense."

"For all we know, Moira could be one of those crazy women who steal other people's kids," said Lucy. "We don't even know for sure that Deirdre is really her child. She could have been abducted. Maybe that's why she's always talking about fairies stealing children."

"Now, Lucy," began Barney. "There's no sense jumping to conclusions."

"I don't think I jumped fast enough," said Lucy. "I feel like a fool. I knew there was something dodgy about Dylan, but I didn't want to face it."

"What do you mean?" asked Barney.

"Well, the morning I met him, when he walked into the

newspaper, he said he was right off the plane from Ireland, with his wife and daughter. But Deirdre said he didn't fly with her and Moira, and when I asked him about it, he, well, he didn't really give me an answer. He just said lots of married people take separate flights."

"They do," said Bill.

"But what if he took an earlier flight, days earlier?" replied Lucy. "Then he could have killed Old Dan."

Barney was skeptical. "His own brother?"

"If he really is his brother. He could be faking," said Lucy. "He could have killed the real Dylan Malone back in Ireland, for that matter. Maybe he even killed Moira and made up the story about the note."

"Lucy," said Bill, getting up and standing behind her so he could wrap his arms around her. "Stop. This isn't productive. You're just making yourself miserable."

"I can't help it," she said, sniffling. "I keep having these horrible thoughts. I'm so scared."

"Me, too," said Bill. "But whatever happens, we'll get through it. Together."

She nodded. "Together," she said as the phone rang.

They turned and stared at it, holding their breaths as Barney picked up the receiver.

"Good," he said, nodding away. "I'll tell them." His face was all smiles. "They've been found. The girls are fine. Everything's okay."

Barney provided an escort, driving his cruiser with the lights flashing and siren blaring, and Bill and Lucy followed in the Subaru, speeding down Red Top Road and on through town, to the police station. Sara and Molly stayed behind, assigned to spread the good news among the neighbors who were still out in the darkening afternoon, searching for the girls.

Barney drove on into the parking lot behind the station, but Bill slipped into a parking space on Main Street, right in front, and they ran inside to the waiting room, where their progress was halted by a sturdy, metal-clad door. Nevertheless, they could hear Moira's voice, which penetrated even the thick, bulletproof Plexiglas that separated the waiting area from the reception desk. They didn't even have time to explain their mission to the officer who was seated there before Barney, who had gone through the rear entrance and opened the door for them. Behind him, in the large office filled with desks and filing cabinets, they only had eyes for Zoe, who was sitting on a chair and holding a can of soda. Lucy ran past the desks and scooped up her daughter, embracing her in a hug. Bill joined them, making what they laughingly called a "Zoe sandwich."

"Stop!" protested Zoe, who wasn't normally allowed to drink soda and was determined to make the most of this opportunity. "I'm going to spill my Coke."

Bill took the can and set it on the chair, and they resumed the hug, squeezing her tighter than before. "I never want to let you go," said Lucy, covering her daughter's face with kisses. "Never, never, ever."

"You're squeezing me," groaned Zoe, trying to wiggle free.

"And I'm going to keep on squeezing you," said Bill. "You gave us an awful scare."

Zoe adopted a puzzled expression. "Why did the policemen bring us here? Did Mrs. Malone do something wrong?"

A high-pitched shriek from Moira distracted them, and Zoe broke loose, reclaiming her seat and her soda.

Bill and Lucy stared at Moira, who was at the center of a group of uniformed and plainclothes officers and was putting on quite a performance. "This is police brutality!" she shouted, stamping her foot and tossing her red curls imperiously. Perhaps reprising a role she had played on stage, she was protectively clutching a very pale and wide-eyed Deirdre to her side. "You had no right stopping me and dragging me here. And the way I've been treated!

Grabbed and shoved! I've had enough! Come on, Deirdre. Let's go."

At this, the officers stepped closer, blocking her way.

"I'm afraid I can't let you go until you've made a statement," said one. "The state police are in charge now, and they want to ask you some questions."

"This is intolerable!" shrieked Moira, eyes blazing. "I'm a woman, a mother." She squeezed Deirdre, who yelped in pain and unsuccessfully tried to free herself from her mother's grip. "You can't treat me like some sort of criminal."

"If you don't calm down, I'll have no choice but to confine you in the lockup." Recognizing the calm, unflappable voice, Lucy turned and saw Detective Horowitz.

"Jail! You can't do that! I haven't been charged with anything. I'm innocent," shouted Moira. She smiled cunningly. "And what about my wee one? Are you going to put her in jail, too?"

"If you don't calm down and start cooperating, I'm going to charge you with kidnapping," said Horowitz. He paused, letting this sink in. "We will make arrangements with social services for the proper care of the child."

"Kidnapping! You can't kidnap your own child," said Moira.

"Actually, you can," said Horowitz. "It happens all the time in custody disputes. And let's not forget the other child in this case. Zoe Stone."

"Right," said Bill, stepping forward. "I think we deserve an explanation."

Now aware of their presence, Moira turned and acknowledged them, rather like a queen receiving her subjects. "I merely took the girls for a drive. A little adventure. I see no harm in it."

"But we didn't know where the children were," protested Lucy. "We were terrified they'd been abducted."

"As it happened, I was rather concerned myself when I

found them all alone and unsupervised," said Moira, narrowing her eyes. "I understood they would be watched by your older daughter."

"They were. Sara only went out for a minute, because the dog ran away," said Lucy.

"It was much longer than a minute," said Moira, self-righteously. "I waited for quite some time, and when she didn't return, I decided I'd better take them both with me. I certainly didn't want to leave little Zoe all by herself. I don't know about you Americans, but in Ireland we take a dim view of leaving young children unattended."

"If you'd waited a few minutes more, I'm sure Sara would have returned," said Lucy. "And, in any case, why didn't you leave a note?"

"It didn't seem necessary," said Moira, with a shrug. "Where else would they be, except with me?"

At this, Lucy lost her temper. "They could have been anywhere! Children are abducted all the time by sexual predators!"

Moira sniffed. "Sexual predators! That's a new one. You Americans are out of your minds. You see sex in everything."

"Don't you realize the trouble you've caused?" asked Horowitz. "There was a three-state alert, and we were about to expand it to the entire New England and mid-Atlantic regions when you were spotted."

"Well, I don't see how any of this was my fault," insisted Moira. "I simply took the girls to the shore for a bit of fresh ocean air."

"We were looking for selkies," volunteered Deirdre.

At this, Zoe chimed in. "And we found one!"

Chapter Twelve

With Zoe safely belted into the backseat of the Subaru, Lucy breathed a sigh of relief as Bill shifted into gear and they headed home, passing Dylan, who was hurrying up the steps to the police station. The sigh turned into a sob as she thought how things might have turned out differently, and the tears stung her eyes.

"Why are you crying now?" asked Bill. "It's all over. Everything's fine."

"I know," said Lucy, wiping her face with a tissue. "It's just . . . well . . . *what if?*"

"Don't think about it," said Bill. He glanced in the rearview mirror, checking on Zoe. "What we need to think about is what to do with a little girl who's been very naughty."

Zoe giggled nervously, and Lucy turned around to face her. "That's right. You gave us an awful scare. Why did you go with Mrs. Malone? You know you're not supposed to go with anyone without permission."

Zoe hung her head. "She said it would be okay, that she was giving permission."

"Mrs. Malone?"

"Yup. She said we would have a big adventure, and you wouldn't want me to miss it."

Hearing this, Lucy felt a surge of anger toward Moira.

What sort of person would persuade a child to disobey her parents?

"Zoe," said Bill in an admonitory tone. "You know better than that. You only get permission from Mommy or me or whoever we leave in charge, like Sara. That's so we know where you are and that you're safe."

Zoe adopted a stubborn expression. "I was safe."

"Yes, but we didn't know that, and we were very worried," said Bill.

"And not just us," said Lucy as they turned onto Red Top Road and started climbing the hill. "Molly and Toby and all the neighbors were worried, too. In fact, they were all out in the wet weather, looking for you."

The news that the girls had been found had spread quickly, and some of the searchers, including Frankie and Willie and all the kids, were standing at the mailboxes at the end of Prudence Path and cheered and waved as they drove by. Zoe, with all the grace of Queen Elizabeth in her glass and gold coach, waved back. Lucy had the uncomfortable feeling that no matter how they scolded or punished Zoe, their cautionary words would be lost among the expressions of joy at her homecoming. Her fears were confirmed when Sara and Molly and Toby all rushed out of the house to meet them in the driveway. The minute Zoe stepped out of the car, she was scooped up in a bear hug by her big brother.

"We saw a selkie!" exclaimed Zoe, triumphantly, as Toby set her down. "It was in the water, and it called to us."

"Don't you mean a seal?" said Lucy, determined to keep her daughter firmly in the here and now.

"No, Mommy," said Zoe, a rebellious little gleam in her eye. "It was definitely a selkie. Deirdre said so, and so did her mother, and they should know, because they come from Ireland, where there are lots of selkies."

"And what exactly is a selkie?" asked Bill.

"I told you," said Zoe in a know-it-all tone. "It's a magical sea creature that helps drowning people get back to shore. But sometimes selkies fall in love with humans, and then they lure them into the sea."

"Hmm," said Toby, skeptically. "If you ask me that's awfully convenient. The selkie gets the credit whether you're saved or you drown."

Zoe glared at him. "You don't understand."

"I think he understands perfectly," said Lucy. "Selkies are make-believe. It's just a story. What you thought was a selkie was a seal."

"That's right, Zoe," said Molly, softly. "You know it was a seal."

"No!" insisted Zoe, sticking out her chin. "It was a selkie."

"That's enough. We're not going to stand out here arguing," said Lucy. "Let's go in the house. And from now on, I don't want you playing with Deirdre."

Reaching the porch, Zoe turned around and faced her mother, who was on the bottom step, at eye level. "That's not fair! I'm going to sleep over with her on Friday night. They've moved out of the hotel and into the uncle's house, and Deirdre has her own room, and she wants me to see it." She paused, adopting a cunning tone. "And you can't stop me, because it's not a school night!"

"School night or not, you're not sleeping over there," said Lucy, mounting the stairs.

Zoe turned around and stamped into the house, pulling off her hat and mittens and jacket and throwing them on the kitchen floor.

"Stop that this instant," said Bill. "Now pick up those things, and hang them up properly."

"I won't!" screamed Zoe, stamping her feet and tossing her head. "You can't make me! You can't make me do anything! I'm going to a sleepover at Deirdre's! I am!" Then she burst into tears and ran up the stairs, where they heard her slam the door to her room.

The rest of the family stood in the kitchen, stunned.

"Was that our Zoe?" asked Bill. "She's never behaved like that before."

"And she's not going to ever again," said Lucy. "Or she's going to be grounded until she's old enough to vote."

When Lucy went to work on Monday, she learned that Ted was planning to run the AMBER Alert as the lead story on page one.

"Can't you bury it inside?" she pleaded. "It's so embarrassing."

"No can do," he told her. "It's the big story this week. The chief isn't about to let it die, either, especially since there's been no progress at all on Old Dan."

"I don't see what all the fuss is about," said Phyllis, who was wearing a fur-trimmed black sweater and dark gray pants. The only bits of color were her magenta fingernails and matching reading glasses, and her tangerine hair. "It isn't like they were really kidnapped. It was all nothing but a silly misunderstanding."

"That's not the point, according to the chief," said Ted. "He says the incident shows the AMBER Alert system works. The girls were located less than ninety minutes after the system was activated."

"It seemed longer than that," said Lucy.

"Nope. He's got the figures, but I can certainly understand how it must have seemed longer to you." Ted paused. "Any chance I can interview Zoe?"

"Absolutely not," said Lucy. "Little Miss Naughty has gotten enough of a swelled head as it is from all the attention she's been getting. Frankie gave her an enormous box of chocolates, Willie Westwood has promised to give her riding lessons, and Preston offered to give her a ride on his ATV."

The thin lines of pencil that served as eyebrows for Phyllis shot up. "You didn't let her go, did you?"

"Of course not, but we paid for it," said Lucy. "Zoe sulked in her room for hours. I swear, the hinges on her door are going to break if she doesn't stop slamming it shut. It's been like living with Sarah Bernhardt ever since I said she couldn't play with Deirdre anymore. She's turned into a real drama queen."

"I think you're doing the right thing," said Ted. "Sometimes you've got to be tough."

"I feel bad about it," admitted Lucy. "She and Deirdre really hit it off. But I can't trust Moira. What kind of mother pulls a stunt like that?"

"If you ask me, the whole family is trouble," said Phyllis. "Old Dan was a piece of work until he got himself beheaded, Moira goes around stealing children, and Dylan is a big show-off. I wish they'd never come to Tinker's Cove."

"Well, that's one way of looking at it," said Ted. "Though I don't think Old Dan beheaded himself."

"I didn't say he did. I said he *got himself* beheaded," said Phyllis. "He must have done something that got somebody awfully mad. He asked for it. Look around. Everybody else in town still has their head, neatly attached, exactly where it ought to be. Not that they all use their heads, I'll give you that, but they've got them. All except Old Dan."

"Point taken," said Ted.

"They never did find his head, did they?" asked Lucy.

"It's probably rolling around in the bottom of the cove," said Ted.

"You'd think it would've turned up by now. Maybe the killer took it," said Lucy.

"That's sick," said Phyllis.

"Where'd you get an idea like that?" asked Ted, managing to sound both shocked and curious.

Lucy shrugged. "I don't know. It just came to me," she said, a bit defensively. "It's not so unusual, if you think about it. I remember visiting the Peabody Essex Museum in Salem with the kids years ago. Toby was around ten then and, boy, was he impressed by the shrunken heads." She shuddered. "Gruesome, evil-looking little things, but I guess they were a popular souvenir with sea captains back in the eighteen hundreds. They brought back a lot of them."

"Their wives probably made them donate them to the museum," speculated Phyllis. "And who could blame them? Who'd want to have a nasty thing like that sitting on the mantel?"

"You know, you've got a point," said Ted, leaning back in his chair. "The English used to display the heads of traitors. They hung them on London Bridge. Left them out for the birds to—"

"Or those terrorists in Iraq," said Lucy. "They're always kidnapping people and beheading them. Even making videotapes and putting them on the Internet."

"Enough," said Phyllis, looking squeamish.

"Oh, get this," said Lucy, who had Googled the word *beheading* and turned up an interesting factoid. "Celtic warriors used to behead their enemies, and then they extracted the brains and mixed them with lime—"

"Stop!" yelled Phyllis, who was looking rather green.

"No, I want to hear this," said Ted, grinning like a kid. "Why'd they do that?"

"To preserve them, I guess," said Lucy as Phyllis covered her ears with her hands. "They made them into little balls, which they carried around with them for bragging rights. Like those shrunken heads at the museum, I guess. The more brain balls you had in your pocket, the braver you were."

"People sure do weird things," said Ted.

"Yeah," agreed Phyllis, who was putting on her coat. "You ever read *Ripley's Believe It or Not!*"

"Not for years," said Ted. "Where are you going?"

"Out for some air," said Phyllis, pushing the door open and making the bell jangle.

"You know, Ted, that's a good idea," said Lucy. "We could run our own strange-but-true column in the paper. Want me to write up the brain balls? Or maybe a sidebar on famous beheadings?"

Lucy knew that Ted was tempted, but in the end, he declined. "We're supposed to be a family newspaper," he said regretfully. "How's that story about the prospectors coming along?"

"Not well," said Lucy. "I could only find one prospector."

"I'd like to run it this week."

"I really don't have enough material for a feature," said Lucy. "And it's not for lack of trying, either. I keep checking the beach, but I only see this one guy. I think the others all went to Florida, where it's warmer and they might find a chest of gold doubloons buried by pirates."

"Go talk to Fred Rumford, at the college," said Ted. "I'm pretty sure one of those prospectors did turn up a gold coin or something a while ago. If I'm not mistaken, he identified it. He'll remember."

"Okay," said Lucy, not displeased with this new assignment. She'd enjoy gossiping with Fred, who was playing Og, the leprechaun, in *Finian's Rainbow*. And besides, the Winchester College Museum was bound to be a lot warmer than the beach.

Winchester College, a small private liberal arts college, was located on the outskirts of town. The campus had plenty of ivy-covered red brick, big old trees, and spacious lawns, but the school's main claim to fame, at least to locals, was the museum, which contained a stuffed mountain lion and a genuine Egyptian mummy. Not that most people ever went there, except for school kids on their annual visit, but if asked to give a special attribute of their town, most Tinker's Cove residents would mention the mummy. The nineteenth-century entrepreneur who had brought it back from a grand tour of Europe and Egypt had intended to experiment with using the linen wrappings to make paper but had been thwarted by an early college president, who also happened to be a Congregationalist minister. He had sermonized against the paper scheme, and the entrepreneur had been left with no option except to donate the mummy to the museum, where it had been sitting in a glass case for more than a hundred years.

Entering the museum, Lucy inhaled the musty scent—a mixture of disinfectant, dust, and overheated air—and paused for a moment to pay her respects to the mummy, as she always did. After all, the mummy, whoever he or she was, had been a person like herself, with likes and dislikes, a family, a job, perhaps even a pet cat, and was a reminder that life ends for everyone and is too precious to be wasted.

"I thought that must be you," said Fred Rumford, popping out of his office. He was the very picture of a college professor, with round tortoise shell eyeglasses, a pale blue oxford cloth shirt, jaunty bow tie, and tweed jacket.

"You don't get too many visitors?" asked Lucy.

"Not this time of year," said Fred. "And you called, so I was expecting you. What can I do for you?"

"I'm doing a feature story about those prospectors with metal detectors. . . ."

He nodded.

"Ted remembers one of them finding an old coin or something a few years ago, which you identified."

"I remember it well. In fact, it's right over here," he said, leading her to a display on the side wall. There she found a surprisingly small gold coin lying in the center of a case, surrounded with photo enlargements and explanations. "It's a British sovereign, dated 1776. We think it must have been dropped by a British soldier. We know troops were marched through Tinker's Cove on their way to fight the rebels in Boston."

Lucy bent down to examine the portrait of George III on the coin, a full-faced gentleman with long, flowing hair. "Was it worth a lot then?"

"A goodly amount, but it's worth a lot more today."

"Who found it?"

"An old fellow named Elmer Howell. That's his picture there." Fred smiled. "He was a neat old guy. He was very proud of the coin."

"Is he still around?" asked Lucy, hoping to interview him.

"Sorry. He died last year. Fortunately for us, he willed the coin to the museum."

"Darn," said Lucy. "Do you mind if I take a picture of the coin?"

"Come on to my office. I have a photo and a fact sheet you can use."

"Great," said Lucy, following him through the door and sitting down in the comfortable armchair he kept for visitors. She looked around his office, which was filled with a fascinating miscellany of objects, ranging from a slab of rock with a dinosaur's footprint to a Navajo rug to a collection of primitive spears, shields, and masks.

Fred opened a file drawer and began flipping through the folders.

"So what do you think of the show? Are you enjoying rehearsals?" asked Lucy.

"I love performing," he said, his fingers pausing on the file tabs. "I've been in every show at the church since they started putting them on fifteen years ago. But this one is different from any of the others I've been in."

"How so?"

"The others were all purely amateur affairs. Everybody

was just out to have a good time. But with Dylan being a professional, it's more high-pressured." He started flipping through the file tabs again. "It's not as much fun."

"Og is a great part," said Lucy.

"A leprechaun who gives up immortality for love," he said, handing her the file. "Pretty improbable, but then the whole story is pretty wild."

"It all works out in the end," said Lucy. " Og gets Susan, Woody gets Sharon, and Finian goes back home to Ireland."

"The script has a happy ending, but I'm not sure this production is going to," said Fred, leaning back in his chair. "Frank and Dylan are always arguing, Moira can't seem to learn her lines, the rehearsals go on forever because they waste so much time, and everybody gets tired. And we only have three more rehearsals before opening night. I can't believe real professional actors and directors behave like this."

"You don't think Dylan is who he says he is?" asked Lucy, encouraged to hear someone else voicing doubts.

"I did in the beginning, but now I'm beginning to wonder," said Fred.

"I'm not even sure he's really Old Dan's brother," said Lucy. "There's no family resemblance that I can see."

"He is quite a bit younger than Old Dan, but that happens. They could even be half brothers."

"Or they might not even be related," said Lucy. "We only have Dylan's word that he was a co-owner of the Bilge, based on papers he produced."

Fred raised an eyebrow. "You think he had some scheme going?"

"I have my suspicions," admitted Lucy.

Fred shrugged. "I dunno. But I'll tell you one thing. I think he, and his wife, too, are both full of blarney, and I'm not the only one who thinks so."

"I think you're right," said Lucy, tucking the file in her bag and standing up. Leaving the museum, she gave the mummy's glass case a little tap, as she always did, for luck. Shamrocks might be lucky, but they were hard to come by in Maine.

Chapter Thirteen

Fred was right, thought Lucy when she arrived at the church hall on Sunday night for rehearsal and found Dylan and Frank embroiled in yet another argument. She was beginning to wonder why she gave up so much of her precious weekend, even missing Sunday dinner, only to sit on an uncomfortable folding chair, waiting for Dylan and Frank to resolve whatever issue they were at odds over and to resume the rehearsal.

Tonight, Pam told her in a whispered voice, it was Og's entrance.

"He should pop out from under the bridge," said Dylan. "That's where leprechauns live, you know, under bridges."

"I think that's trolls," said Frank. "He doesn't have time to get under the bridge. It would work better for him to pop out from behind a tree."

"He's not a bloody jack-in-the-box," declared Dylan in ringing tones. "He's a leprechaun, and everybody knows leprechauns live under bridges."

"Maybe everybody knows that in Ireland, but here in Maine, I don't think they'll care. We've only got a bar and a half of music to get him on stage, and if we play around with a spotlight for a bit, it will build suspense. . . ."

"Ah, but if there's only a bar and a half of music, which

leaves no time for him to hide, why would we have time to mess around with a spotlight, can you tell me that?"

"That's why we need the spotlight," said Frank, sighing. "It solves a bunch of problems. It gives Og some extra time to get in place, and it will heighten the dramatic effect of his entrance. The audience will love it."

Hearing this, Dylan's eyebrows shot up, and he glared at Frank. "Ah, so you say it will heighten the dramatic effect, do you? Since when exactly did you become the drama expert here? Do you know who you're talking to? I think I can claim to have more dramatic experience than you, having performed on stages throughout the British Isles, including the Old Vic and Dublin's own Abbey Theatre."

"Yeah, well, I checked these so-called credits of yours and discovered you were a spear-carrier in a show the *Daily Mail* called 'Shakespearean in title only' and 'a muddled mishmash that would make the Bard blush.' "

Hearing this, Lucy pricked up her ears and listened intently as Frank continued in a scathing tone. "And your turn at the Abbey Theatre was as narrator for a children's puppet show. You read your lines offstage. And, as for that TV series, you were in one episode, and you got killed in the first two minutes."

"I was featured throughout—"

"As a corpse," sneered Frank. "All you had to do was remember not to sneeze."

Lucy wasn't the only one paying attention; most of the cast members were following the exchange.

"Spite," said Dylan, spitting out the word. "Spite and jealousy. That's what motivates you, and it's a sad thing to see."

"I've had just about enough of this," said Fred, who had been waiting to take direction. "We're wasting time. I say I go behind the tree, because, to tell the truth, I'm six two and

I just had knee surgery and I don't think I can get under that bridge without tearing my meniscus all over again."

"Good enough," said Frank, striding to the piano and hitting a chord. "Places everyone."

"Don't ever do that again," hissed Dylan. "I'm the director, and I tell the cast when to take their places."

"Well, then, do it," snarled Frank. "These people have jobs. A lot of them work on weekends, you know. They can't sleep all morning, like some people."

"Directing is exhausting work," said Moira, taking her place center stage as Og slipped behind the plywood tree trunk and the chorus members drifted onstage. "Dylan needs the recuperative benefits of at least ten hours of sleep, as do I."

"Ten hours of sleep," murmured Lucy to Pam as they joined the others onstage. "Now I really hate her."

Pam chuckled. "Somewhere along the line we went wrong. We should have structured our lives differently."

"You said it," agreed Lucy. "Starting tomorrow, the girls can make their own breakfast and get themselves off to school, Bill can make his own lunch, and the dog can let herself out. I'm going to catch up on my sleep."

"Right," said Pam, clearly not believing a word of it.

"You'll see," insisted Lucy. "Tell Ted I'll be in around noon."

"You tell him yourself," said Pam. "I'm not going—"

"Ladies! Do you mind?" snapped Frank, fixing his eyes on them. "We'll start with 'Something Sort of Grandish' with Og and Sharon, and then we'll segue right into 'Necessity.' " He raised his voice. "Sharon. We need you."

Moira, who had drifted backstage, ignored him, deeply engrossed in conversation with Dave Reilly.

"Moira!" Frank called again. "You need the practice, dear, and since Og is doing 'Something Sort of Grandish,' you might as well sing along, too."

Moira shrugged and turned slowly, swiveling her hips. "If you say so, Frank." All eyes were on her as she walked across the stage, right into the path of Tatiana, who was practicing turns. The collision was inevitable.

"Bitch! You did that on purpose!" shrieked Moira, shoving Tatiana, who landed awkwardly on her bottom.

"I'm so sorry. I didn't see you, really," said the dancer, scrambling to her feet and dusting herself off.

"Liar!" said Moira. "Face it, you can't stand the fact that Dave likes me better than you. You'd do anything to get me out of the way."

"Face it yourself, Moira. Dave doesn't like you at all. He's just being polite," said the dance teacher, coolly. "You're the last person I would be jealous of, believe me."

"Well, if you're not jealous, why do you always have it out for me?"

"Look who's talking! I've been working on this combination for at least fifteen minutes, right here. You walked right into my path."

"You went out of your way to knock into me," said Moira. "Ask anyone."

The chorus members cast their eyes in a dozen different directions, all avoiding eye contact with Moira. In Pam's case, it didn't work.

"You saw, didn't you, Pam?" said Moira. "She changed direction and ran right into me."

"Don't ask me," said Pam. "I didn't actually see what happened."

"Well, what about you, Harry?" demanded Moira, selecting the harbormaster to press her point.

Harry shrugged and rolled his eyes. "Can we get on with the rehearsal?" he asked. "I've got to get up at four tomorrow to catch a plane."

"Right," said Frank, banging out a chord. "From the top."

Relieved to finally be doing something, the chorus members put their hearts into their singing, winning approving nods and smiles from Frank, until Moira missed her cue.

"Moira, dear," he hissed, "you're supposed to come in here." He pounded out the chord on the piano.

"Oh, right," she said, singing the wrong lyrics in the wrong key.

Frank slammed down the lid on the keyboard. "Enough! I've had it!" he yelled at Dylan. "What is the point? She won't learn the words; she won't practice the songs; she doesn't even pay attention!"

Dylan, who had been sitting along the side of the room, with his knees crossed, studying the script, slowly got up. He nodded slowly, a benign smile on his face, and spoke slowly, as if speaking to an idiot. "True talent like Moira's needs nurturing. It needs tender care, respect, and admiration in order to blossom."

"How about some respect for me? For everyone here?" demanded Frank.

"I think it would be best if we called it a night," said Dylan, with a shrug. "Everyone's tired."

"Call it a night! We haven't even got through the second act, and there's only two more rehearsals before opening night!" said Frank.

Dylan shrugged. "We'll schedule some extra rehearsals," he said. "Meanwhile, I have an important announcement."

They all stood in place reluctantly, shuffling their feet and eager to be on their way.

"I know how very frustrating and tiring rehearsals can be," he began, "but I want to assure you that all your hard work and sacrifice will be rewarded on opening night, when we will have a very special guest."

He paused, letting them speculate for a few moments.

"I have just received word that Lieutenant Governor Cormac O'Donnell will attend himself, in person."

Moira clapped her hands together in excitement, but the rest of the cast showed little reaction.

"I thought there'd be more enthusiasm," said Dylan. "He is the lieutenant governor, after all. And from what I hear, he's very proud of his Irish heritage."

"Well, if you want excitement, you'll have to get Mikey O'Donnell," said Harry, getting a big laugh.

"Good one, Harry," said Frank.

"Who's Mikey?" asked Dylan. "How do we get him?"

"That's what a lot of people want to know. Cormac's brother Michael is on the FBI's Ten Most Wanted list," said Frank.

"I don't believe it," said Moira, casting a look at her husband. "The lieutenant governor's brother is a criminal?"

"A gangster," said Frank. "Every once in a while, you read something about him in the paper, turning up in Italy or London. They never seem to be able to catch him, though."

"What do they want him for?" asked Moira.

"Racketeering, murder, extortion, you name it," said Harry.

"So one's a politician and the other is a criminal?" asked Moira.

"Not really that different, after all," said Harry, getting another big laugh.

Lucy was laughing along with the rest when her cell phone rang, and she scurried across the room to the chair where she'd left her coat and purse. After a few awkward moments, she found it in her coat pocket and flipped it open.

"Mom?" said Toby, his voice shaky, through the static.

Lucy immediately knew something was the matter. "I'm here," she said, moving toward the window. "What's the matter?"

"I'm at the hospital with Molly," he said.

Lucy did a quick calculation. Molly wasn't due for another six weeks.

"She started bleeding," added Toby.

"How's she doing?"

"I dunno, Mom." His voice trailed off, his words lost, then came back. "I'm really worried."

"I'll be right there," said Lucy.

Breaking her rule not to talk on the phone while driving, she called Bill as she speeded straight for the Tinker's Cove Cottage Hospital. There she found Toby sitting on an orange vinyl chair in the emergency-room waiting area. He was a strapping kid, well over six feet tall, but he looked small and frightened sitting there all alone.

"Any news?" she asked, and he stood up, shaking his head. "It will be okay," she said, giving him a big hug. "She's in good hands."

It was at least another hour before Doc Ryder finally came out to talk to them. He was not only the family doctor; he had delivered all four of Lucy's babies, including Toby.

"Sorry to keep you waiting so long," he said. "We're shorthanded tonight."

"How's Molly?" asked Toby.

"We've got the bleeding stopped, but I don't like her blood pressure," said Doc Ryder.

None of this made any sense to Toby. "How's the baby?" he asked.

"So far, so good," said Doc Ryder.

"Can I take Molly home?" asked Toby.

"Son," said the doctor, putting a hand on his shoulder, "I'm afraid not. Not until we get her blood pressure under control."

"How long will that take?" asked Toby.

"As long as it takes," said the doctor.

"Can I see her?" Toby asked.

"If you promise not to upset her."

"I won't. I promise."

The doctor nodded. "And make it quick."

"I will," replied Toby.

When Toby was gone, the doctor told Lucy to take a seat. He sat down heavily next to her and shook his head. Lucy waited with dread to hear what he had to say.

"It's not good," he said. "Even if we manage to get her blood pressure down, she'll have to stay on bed rest."

"For how long?"

"The longer the better. Toxemia's a waiting game. We want to keep her from going into labor as long as we can, get that baby as close to term as we can."

Lucy didn't know much about toxemia except that it didn't sound good. "But if her blood pressure stays up?"

"We'll have to take the baby, even if it's early."

"How big is the baby now?"

"Not as big as I'd like. Maybe four pounds. That's my best guess."

Lucy thought of the premies she'd seen in photos and on TV. Little tiny creatures with wizened faces and stick arms and legs, covered with thin, wrinkled red skin. They had the unfinished, prehistoric look of newly hatched birds, before their feathers came out.

"Don't worry," he said, patting her knee. "If it's just a question of the baby being early, we've got excellent facilities right here."

"And if something is wrong?"

"Well, there's the neonatal unit in Portland. They can do amazing stuff nowadays. They can even repair heart valves, all sorts of stuff, with the baby in utero."

"This is supposed to reassure me?" asked Lucy.

"I just want you to be prepared, that's all. Those kids will be looking to you for support," he said, getting to his feet slowly and stretching. "I guess he's been in there long enough."

He walked off stiffly, as if his back was bothering him. A minute or two later, Toby came out of the treatment room and sat beside her. He didn't look much happier than when he went in.

"How's she doing?" asked Lucy.

"She's scared, Mom." He sat with his elbows resting on his knees and looked down at his hands. "I'm scared, too."

"It will be okay," she told him, echoing the doctor's words. "They have good facilities here and even better in Portland, if they're needed. Right now the doctor says it's a waiting game. All we can do is wait."

And wait they did, all through the night. Molly's condition was unchanged when Lucy left the hospital at six in the morning. She wanted to make breakfast for Bill and the girls and get their day off to a good start. Then she planned to catch an hour or two of sleep and take a shower before going back to the hospital. She shook her head ruefully, thinking of her flippant assertion the night before that she was going to sleep for ten hours, like Moira.

The house was quiet when she entered. Only Libby, the dog, greeted her, rising from her doggy bed in the kitchen and sticking out her front legs in a stretch, yawning and shaking before beginning her usual tail-wagging, wiggly welcome. Lucy gave her a pat and let her out, then got the coffeemaker started. She called the dog back into the house, filled her bowl with kibble, and then went upstairs to wake the family.

Back downstairs, she poured herself a cup of coffee and sipped at it while she got some bacon cooking and made lunches for Bill and Zoe. Sara insisted on buying the school lunch, but Lucy suspected she skipped it and saved the money. Too much caffeine and worry had made her feel shaky, and since she had more time than usual this morning, she decided to make French toast. She needed a hearty breakfast, and it would be a treat for Bill and the girls.

"Mmm, that sure smells good," said Bill, the first one to appear. "So how's Molly?" he asked as Lucy filled a mug with coffee and gave it to him.

"Her blood pressure is dangerously high, and they can't seem to get it down."

"What does that mean?" he asked, sitting at the table.

Lucy kept it simple. "Bed rest if they can get it down, an emergency caesarean if not."

Bill took a swallow of coffee. "When will they know?"

"By noon. Doc Ryder promised a decision by then." She took a deep breath and let out a quavery sigh, which caught Bill's attention. She covered with a yawn. "I'm going to nap for an hour or so, then go back to the hospital."

"How's Toby?"

"Really scared." This time her voice did crack, and she made herself very busy filling a pitcher with maple syrup.

"Poor guy."

Lucy set a platter full of bacon and French toast on the table and yelled up the stairs, calling the girls. They came clumping down together. Lucy felt like scooping them up in a big hug but restrained herself. They'd think she'd lost her mind.

"Ooh, yummy," said Zoe, spotting the French toast.

"Just juice for me," said Sara.

"Do me a favor and have a piece," said Lucy, seizing on the distraction. Arguing with Sara was better than worrying. "It's not that many calories if you skip the butter and syrup. Dab some yogurt on instead."

"Half a piece," said Sara.

"How's Molly?" asked Zoe. "Can I go there after school?"

"Sorry, honey. She's still in the hospital," said Bill.

"How come?" asked Zoe, her mouth full of French toast.

"She's sick, and they have to take special care of her and the baby," he answered.

Sara, Lucy noticed, was reaching for a second piece of French toast. "But everything's going to be okay, right?" she asked.

"We hope so," said Lucy, her throat catching again.

The girls caught it and looked at her anxiously, watching as she filled her plate. Her hand shook, and she dropped a piece of bacon on the floor. Libby, who had been waiting for just such an opportunity, gobbled it up.

"Sally Henderson's mom had a high-risk pregnancy, but everything turned out all right," said Sara. "She just had to stay in bed at the end."

"That's what Molly should do," said Zoe. "If she stays inside, the wee folk won't be able to get her baby."

Lucy dropped her fork, and it clattered to the floor. "It's not wee folk that are making Molly sick," she said, through clenched teeth. "I don't want to hear any more about fairies or selkies or leprechauns, do you understand? Molly is sick, that's all there is to it, and she's going to get better and have a healthy baby."

Zoe said, "But Deirdre told me that the fairies can make mothers sick. . . ."

"Enough!" screamed Lucy, jumping to her feet. "I don't want to hear any more of this!" She picked up her plate and took it over to the counter, where she began filling the dishwasher.

"Zoe," said Bill, his voice calm, "we talked about this before. There is no such thing as fairies. People get sick for lots of reasons, but fairies have nothing to do with it. They're imaginary. Make-believe. And your mother and I don't want to hear another word about them."

Zoe's face closed up, and she got up from the table. "I don't want to miss the bus," she said. She put on her coat and packed her lunch in her backpack and went out without kissing her mother good-bye. Lucy stood at the kitchen sink, watching through the window as Zoe walked slowly down the driveway. She looked exactly like someone who'd lost her best friend. Lucy sighed and glanced at the clock.

"You'd better hurry, Sara," she said.

When they were both gone, she sat down at the table, where Bill was working on a second cup of coffee.

"I shouldn't have yelled at her," she said. "She's grief-stricken."

He shrugged. "She knows you're upset about Molly."

"I'll apologize when she gets home from school."

"I bet she'll have forgotten all about it by then."

"I doubt it." Lucy exhaled. "I wish she'd forget about fairies."

"It's too bad. She had a nice friendship going with Deirdre."

"She really misses her."

"If only Deirdre didn't come with a whole retinue of wee folk," said Bill, chuckling.

"Maybe I could talk to Moira mother to mother and get her to tell Zoe that it's all make-believe."

"Have Deirdre keep the sprites and elves at home," said Bill, smiling. "And the girls can only play here, under your supervision."

"Right," said Lucy. "We'll get her hooked on video games and rap music." She smiled for the first time that morning. "How's that for revenge?"

Chapter Fourteen

When Lucy got back to the hospital, she found Molly had been moved out of the emergency room and was comfortably settled all by herself in a semiprivate room with a stunning view of the harbor.

"Nice digs," said Lucy, giving her a peck on the cheek. Today Molly's face was even more puffy and swollen, which Lucy knew was a symptom of toxemia. She'd looked it up on Google before leaving the house that morning. It hadn't made for encouraging reading.

"It looks as if I'm going to be here for a while," said Molly. "Doc Ryder says I'll probably have to stay here until the baby is born."

Lucy had expected as much. "How do you feel?"

"Stupid," said Molly, shaking her head ruefully. "I thought all this swelling was just part of pregnancy. I didn't know it meant something's wrong."

"Don't blame yourself," said Lucy. "I've had four kids, and I didn't know about it until I looked it up on the computer this morning." She paused, looking out the window and watching a seagull circling against the blue sky. "It could have been a lot worse."

"I know." Molly stroked her big stomach. "They say the baby's okay, but I have to stay here so they can monitor my blood pressure. If it goes up again, they'll do a

C-section." She shrugged. "That's not so bad. Lots of people actually choose caesareans these days."

Lucy nodded and squeezed her hand. Apparently, Doc Ryder hadn't told her the whole story. That the baby was compromised because of the toxemia, and that Molly herself was at risk of convulsions, organ damage, and even coma.

"Everything will be fine," said Lucy, trying to reassure herself as well as Molly. "You must do exactly what they tell you. Now, what can I bring you? Books? Magazines? Knitting?"

"Nothing right now. Toby promised to go to the library and get me a bunch of books. Meanwhile, I've got the TV. And I'll probably sleep some," she said, yawning.

Lucy took the hint. "I'd better go, then. I'll be back tonight."

Lucy left, intending to get a pretty nightgown for Molly to replace the hospital gown, and stopped at the nurse's station to check that she could wear them.

"No problem," said the nurse.

"How's she doing—really?" asked Lucy.

"I'm not supposed to discuss a patient's condition," she said, leaning over the counter, "but, well, she reminds me of my own daughter, and she's so young. She's going to need a lot of support."

Hearing this, Lucy was suddenly ashamed that she had been so critical earlier, fretting over the fact that Molly and Toby weren't married. Now that didn't seem so important. "We'll be here for them, that's for sure," promised Lucy.

"This is one of those touch and go situations that can change in an instant."

"I was afraid of that," said Lucy.

"We're keeping a real close eye on her," said the nurse. "Try not to worry."

"Sure," said Lucy.

Leaving the hospital, she knew that worry was going to be a constant companion until Molly was safely delivered of a healthy baby. No matter how often she shoved it aside to think of something else, it would come right back, catching her when she least expected it. No, worry was going to be around for a while.

Lucy had called Ted earlier and knew he wasn't expecting her to come to work until later in the day, if at all, so she decided she might as well pay a visit to the Malones and tackle the fairy issue. She was having enough trouble dealing with real problems; she didn't need made-up ones.

She'd heard that they had moved out of the inn and taken possession of Old Dan's bungalow right after the funeral, so she headed for Bumps River Road, on the other side of town. Unlike most of Tinker's Cove, where the historical commission made sure everyone conformed to strict guidelines of "appropriateness" when it came to paint color, roof shingles, and even light fixtures, and comprehensive zoning regulations restricted new development, Bumps River Road was an uncontrolled mix of small businesses, like auto body shops and landscape outfits, with a scattering of ramshackle houses, all tucked in around the town dump. The area had actually improved in recent years, ever since the smelly dump had been converted into a transfer station, where trash was collected and shipped to a regional disposal facility. Lucy occasionally missed the old dump, where the rule that one man's trash was another's treasure meant that you often took home as much as you left, but she didn't miss the enormous flock of seagulls that converged as soon as you backed up to the edge of the pit, squabbling over your garbage even before it hit bottom.

Some of the businesses on the road had taken their cue from the neatly landscaped transfer station and had fixed up their places, applying fresh paint, installing fences and security lights, spreading blacktop for parking, and even laying down a few strips of loam and a bush or two. A few of the houses had been rehabbed in recent years, too, but not Old Dan's bungalow.

It was set apart from the others, down a winding dirt driveway. Pine saplings and scraggly low-bush blueberries were filling in the unkempt yard, where a couple of rusty automobile carcasses were rotting away on cement blocks, the tires having been thriftily removed and probably sold. The house had also been neglected. There the paint peeled from the window frames, the porch sagged, and the roof shingles that hadn't blown away were cupped and curling. A straggly tree stood in the yard. Limbs broken in winter storms dangled down dangerously, and a few crows called noisily from their precarious perches in the very topmost branches.

The derelict bungalow was so unwelcoming, and the caws of the crows so harsh, that Lucy almost decided not to stop but to go right on home. Appearances were deceiving, she reminded herself. Dylan and Moira couldn't be blamed for Old Dan's slovenliness; indeed, on closer inspection, she saw the windows had recently been washed, as had the curtains, and the brass doorknob polished. A brand-new welcome mat had even been laid on the rotting porch. Somewhat reassured, she got out of her car, mounted the sagging steps to the porch, and knocked on the door.

At the sound, the crows rose from the tree and flapped around, making a terrific racket with their caws. Watching from the shelter of the porch, Lucy couldn't decide which was worse: their noisy squawks or their silent, brooding watchfulness when they settled back onto their roosts. She liked birds well enough. She even set out a bird feeder in winter and enjoyed watching the chickadees and nuthatches and cardinals, which were regular visitors. She even liked blue jays, admiring their bright blue feathers and cocky attitude, but she didn't like crows. They were too smart, too aggressive, and altogether too nasty, with their habit of snatching other birds' helpless hatchlings from their nests and gobbling them up.

Getting no answer from inside, Lucy tapped again on the glass pane in the door, then cupped her hands around her eyes and peered in. This time the crows remained quiet, but she could see their reflections in the glass, their dark, beaky shapes silhouetted against the bright sky. Now that they had settled down and stopped cawing, she became aware of an eerie wailing sound. Pressing her hands tighter against the glass, Lucy strained to see inside the house. As her eyes adjusted, she finally was able to make out a kneeling figure. It was Moira kneeling over Dylan, who was lying flat on the floor, keening as she had at Old Dan's funeral.

Lucy tried the knob and discovered the door was unlocked, so she let herself in and rushed to Moira's side, where she quickly assessed the situation. Dylan was sprawled on his back, apparently felled by a blow to his forehead. There was an enormous amount of blood, but Lucy was encouraged when she felt Dylan's wrist and found a weak, fluttering pulse.

"He's alive, Moira. We have to get help."

Moira didn't react but kept on keening, rocking back and forth over her husband.

Lucy pulled her cell phone out of her pocket and dialed 911. Reassured that help was on the way, she turned to Moira, grabbing her by the shoulders and shaking her. "What happened, Moira?" she shouted. "Tell me what happened."

Moira didn't respond; she just kept on rocking and wailing, apparently in a state of shock. Lucy doubted she even knew she was there.

The wail of the siren as the ambulance came tearing down the driveway and the arrival of the EMTs shattered the spell, and Moira suddenly snapped out of her trance.

"Ohmigod, ohmigod," she shrieked. "Leave him be."

"Moira, they've come to help," said Lucy. "He's alive."

"He is?" she asked, eyes wide.

"Yes. See. They're putting an oxygen mask on him to help him breathe. He's breathing. He's bleeding. That's a good sign."

"Blood! Blood!" she shrieked, tossing her head back and throwing up her hands. "So much blood!"

Lucy was losing patience with Lady Macbeth, or whomever Moira was playing, but the EMTs were unmoved by her dramatics. "Head wounds bleed a lot," said one, speaking in a matter-of-fact tone to Moira. "Are you his wife?"

"That I am, and what a terrible thing it was to find him like this," said, Moira, clasping her hands together as if in prayer.

The EMT continued. "His vital signs are pretty strong, but we won't know what's what until we get him to the hospital and they do a CAT scan. Do you want to ride in the ambulance with him?"

"I'll drive her," volunteered Lucy. "That way she'll have a ride home."

With that, they hoisted the still-unconscious Dylan onto a stretcher and wheeled him out of the house to the ambulance. Lucy found Moira's cloak hanging from a hook beside the door and draped it over her shoulders, then led her by the arm out of the house to the car. As she was starting the car, she remembered Deirdre. The little girl couldn't be in the house, could she?

"Where's Deirdre?" she asked Moira.

"With Dave Reilly. She loves helping him paint the scenery."

"You'd better call him and ask him to keep her," advised Lucy. "Do you need my cell phone?"

"No, I have one," said Moira, hesitating a moment before opening it. Dave Reilly's number was the first in the address book.

*   *   *

Once again, Lucy found herself sitting on an uncomfortable chair in the waiting area at the emergency room. This was getting to be a bad habit, she thought, casting a glance at Moira. She was sitting on the edge of her seat, anxiously awaiting the doctor's report on her husband's condition. Lucy wasn't entirely convinced that she wasn't playacting but tried not to pursue that train of thought. Instead, she asked her about Old Dan. It seemed too much of a coincidence that one brother was attacked so soon after the other's violent death.

"I would never have guessed your husband and Old Dan were brothers," said Lucy. "They seem so different. Were they close?"

Moira shrugged. "Well, Daniel moved to America some time ago."

"But now with cheap long distance and e-mail, it's easy to keep in touch."

"I suppose they did. I never paid much attention. Why do you ask?"

"I'm thinking of doing a story on far-flung families for the paper," said Lucy, who hadn't really been intending to do any such thing but, now that she'd thought of it, was thinking it was a pretty good idea, after all.

"Daniel was quite a bit older than Dylan," said Moira. "He'd already emigrated before Dylan was born."

"But they were partners in the Bilge?"

"There was a bit of money when their mother died. I think that's what it was. Daniel offered to sell Dylan a half interest in the business for his share of the inheritance. It seemed like a good deal for us."

"Did they have any enemies?" asked Lucy.

"Old Dan must have," said Moira. "But everybody loves my Dylan."

"Not quite everybody," said Lucy. "Somebody disliked him enough to conk him on the head."

Moira narrowed her eyes, and Lucy wondered if she had an idea who might have attacked her husband, but if she did, she kept the thought to herself. Lucy was about to question her when the door swung open and Doc Ryder appeared. "Lucy!" he exclaimed. "We've got to stop meeting like this."

"No kidding," said Lucy. "I came with Moira, Dylan's wife."

"I'm Doctor Ryder," he said, taking Moira's hand. "I just examined your husband."

"Will he be all right?" asked Moira, clinging to his hand and whispering.

Doc Ryder covered her hand, now holding it with both of his. Lucy felt like groaning. You'd think a doctor would be able to resist Moira's charms.

"I wish I had better news for you," he said.

Moira gasped.

"Now, now," he continued quickly. "I didn't mean to frighten you. He's a strong man, and he's holding his own. He has at least a fifty-fifty chance of a full recovery. Maybe more. I've spoken to the best brain man in the state, and we're going to transfer your husband to University Hospital, where they have a lot more experience with head injuries." He paused, shaking his head. "I've never seen anything like this in forty years of practice. The stone that hit him is lodged in the wound."

"It's still there?" asked Lucy, incredulous.

Doc Ryder nodded. "I didn't dare touch it. This is one for the experts."

Moira, who had gone quite pale, sat down and crossed herself. "May the saints preserve us," she said, clasping her hands together and looking over her shoulders. "Evil forces are at work here."

Lucy grabbed her by the shoulders and looked her in the eye. "Moira, if you know what this is about, you need to tell the police."

Moira shook her head. "The police can't do anything. My poor Dylan is in a fight for his soul, just like King Conor."

"Who's he?" asked Lucy.

"King Conor Mac Nessa? A saint. He was hit in the head, just like my Dylan, and the doctors left the projectile in place, fearing it would be fatal to remove it. So there it stayed, and King Conor was fine until one dark day, when the Druid priests came and told him they had seen visions of a truly good man crucified on a cross of wood. It was Christ, you see. And the tale so horrified King Conor that his head exploded and he died."

"Well, never fear. There's no danger of that happening to your husband," said Doc Ryder in a disapproving tone. "We're keeping him under anesthesia."

"King Conor was a handsome man, just like my husband," said Moira. "Will my Dylan be disfigured?"

"That's the least of his worries right now," said the doctor, bluntly. Then, remembering his bedside manner, he added, "It's amazing what these plastic surgeons can do nowadays."

"That's a relief," said Moira, with a sigh.

"Would you like to see him before we move him?" asked the doctor.

Before Moira could answer, Dave Reilly came through the door, holding little Deirdre by the hand. At the same time, a couple of uniformed cops who Lucy had seen at the house exited from the elevator, carrying paper cups of coffee from the hospital cafeteria.

Jumping to her feet, Moira ran across the waiting room and snatched her daughter from Dave, dramatically clasping her to her bosom. Finding her rather heavier than she'd expected, she dropped her and, raising her arm and pointing at Dave, screamed, "Murtherer! You tried to kill my husband!"

All eyes—the cops', Doc Ryder's, Lucy's, Deirdre's, even

those of the women at the admissions desk—were on Dave, who stood frozen in place, with a puzzled expression on his face.

"I don't know what you're talking about," he said.

"Don't pretend!" shrieked Moira, shaking off Deirdre, who was attempting to hug her. "You were jealous! Admit it. You knew he'd never let me go, so you killed him!"

"He's not dead," reminded Doc Ryder.

"You're crazy," said Dave, addressing Moira.

"Look, buddy," said one of the cops, "mebbe we better have a little talk."

Chapter Fifteen

"She's crazy," protested Dave. "I don't even know what she's talking about."

"Let go of my child, you murtherer!" shrieked Moira.

Clearly terrified by all the screaming, Deirdre clung tightly to Dave's hand. He bent down and whispered in her ear, urging her to go to her mother, but she only stepped closer to him. This enraged Moira even more, and she flew at the child, grabbing her by the arm and pulling her away from Dave. The tug-of-war continued, with Deirdre hanging on to Dave and Moira pulling her other arm, until she finally succeeded in yanking her free. She then enfolded the mute child in her arms and began to sob dramatically into her hair.

"My precious! I dread to think what might have happened!" cried Moira.

The cops looked at each other, seemingly unsure what to do. They were saved from having to take action by the arrival of Detective Horowitz, who huddled with the two officers, questioning them and glancing in turn at Moira, Dave, little Deirdre, and finally, Lucy.

"Come with me," said Horowitz, pointing at Lucy. "You two, and the child, can take a seat," he continued, speaking to Dave and Moira. "And don't get any ideas about leaving, because these two fine officers have orders to keep you here until I tell them otherwise."

Dave settled down, propping his elbows on his knees and resting his chin in his hands, but Moira protested at the top of her voice. "This is outrageous," she screamed. "You can't expect me to stay here with the man who murthered my husband!"

"He's still alive," Horowitz reminded her. Then he took Lucy's elbow and steered her down the hallway. "Is she always like this?" he asked under his breath.

"She's an actress," said Lucy. "She has a flair for the dramatic."

"But not for calling nine-one-one when she finds her husband unconscious and bleeding?" he asked.

"I think she really thought he was dead," said Lucy. "She was wailing and cradling him in her arms when I found them."

"I think the lady doth protest a bit too much," said Horowitz. "What's the deal with the long-haired guy?"

"Dave Reilly? He's the leading man in the church show, *Finian's Rainbow*. Moira, of course, is the lead female. They're lovers onstage, and it's pretty clear Moira would like to take the affair offstage, too, but I don't know if Dave is all that interested. He plays in a rock band. He can pretty much have any girl he wants—and they're a lot younger than Moira."

"Meow," said Horowitz, a twinkle in his eye. "Do I detect a bit of cattiness?"

Lucy felt her cheeks warming. "I wish I'd never gotten involved with that woman, or her little kid. She's convinced my Zoe that fairies and leprechauns and I don't know what all lurk under every tree. We haven't had a decent night's sleep since they arrived."

Horowitz scratched his chin. "So why exactly did you go to their house this morning?"

"It was a stupid idea, probably, but I was hoping to

convince Moira to tell Zoe that the fairies were make-believe, that they were just storybook characters. I thought if Zoe heard it from the source, instead of her parents, she'd come around and give up all this nonsense and get back to normal."

"And did she agree?"

"I never got a chance to ask her. She was holding Dylan in her arms and wailing, and I took one look and called for help."

"Do you have any idea how long he'd been like that?"

"It couldn't have been too long, because he was still bleeding." Lucy shook her head. "I don't even know what time it was when I got there."

"You didn't see anybody else?"

"Sorry," she said. "Not a soul."

Horowitz nodded. "Not to worry. You've been very helpful." Then he turned, starting to go back down the hall, but Lucy put her hand on his arm, detaining him. "How come you're being so nice to me?" she asked.

"Well, for once, you're not playing the amateur detective, and you did the right thing. You called for help." He grimaced. "You probably saved his life."

Lucy smiled. "Will I get a medal?"

"Don't push it," he growled, marching off down the hall.

Lucy followed, casually taking a seat on the opposite side of the waiting area and hoping no one would notice she was there. She pulled her cell phone out of her purse and opened it, pretending to check her messages while she listened in on Horowitz's conversation with Dave and Moira.

He began by questioning Dave. "Where were you this morning?" he demanded, getting right to the point.

"At home."

"And where's that?"

"The new condos on Bumps River Road." At this, Lucy

perked up. The condos were just down the road from Old Dan's place.

"Oh yeah, the affordable housing?"

Dave nodded. "I entered the lottery and got one."

"That's not far from the victim's home, right?"

Dave nodded.

"Handy, especially if you're having an affair with the victim's wife."

Dave laughed. "Affair? I don't think so. I was the baby-sitter."

"Baby-sitter?"

"Moira came banging on my door around nine this morning. Woke me up. I had a gig last night, didn't get home until three, and then with one thing and another, it must've been close to four when I got to bed. So I was sound asleep when she starts pounding on the door and ringing the bell. Said she wanted me to take the kid 'cause she had something she had to do. Then she shoved the kid through the door and was gone before I had a chance to say anything."

"That's ridic—" sputtered Moira, but she was silenced by a glance from Horowitz.

"So what'd you do then?" he asked Dave.

"I put the TV on for the kid while I took a shower and got dressed. Then I made some coffee and I watched a few cartoons with the kid and then I decided to take her back." He glanced at Moira. "I was sick and tired of being used like that. But nobody was home when I got there, just a cop who was putting up yellow crime-scene tape. He told me they were at the hospital, so I came here."

"Okay," said Horowitz, turning to Moira. "What was the hurry? Why did you take your child to his place? What were you going to do this morning?"

"I had a hair appointment."

Horowitz hadn't expected this. "What?"

"You woke me up so you could get a haircut?" demanded Dave.

"Not just a hair appointment, an appointment with Jean-Pierre," said Moira.

In her corner, Lucy was impressed. It was practically impossible to get an appointment with Jean-Pierre himself, who owned a salon in the fancy new galleria that had been built just a few exits away on the interstate.

"I knew I couldn't be late, and my usual baby-sitter had quit, so I really didn't have any other option, did I?" said Moira.

Lucy had a feeling she was the "usual baby-sitter" Moira was referring to, and she didn't like it much. The woman had a lot of nerve, referring to her like an employee, when she had simply offered to let Deirdre play with Zoe when it was convenient for both families.

"Your husband couldn't have stayed with the child?" asked Horowitz.

"Oh no. He's directing a play, and he couldn't be distracted."

"So you left the house around nine?"

"Right. The appointment was at ten, and I'm not familiar with the area, so I wanted to leave plenty of time to get there."

Horowitz consulted his notebook. "But at some point you went back to the house. How come?"

"I remembered I forgot my credit card, so I went back home to get it, and that's when"—she dabbed at her eyes and sniffed—"I found my darling husband."

"What time was that?"

Moira's eyes blazed. "I don't know what time it was! My husband was lying on the floor. There was blood everywhere. I thought he was dead, for pity's sake." She paused dramatically. "I didn't check my watch."

Horowitz raised his eyes, meeting hers. "You didn't call

for help, but you did remember to cancel the hair appointment."

Hearing this, Lucy's jaw dropped in shock.

"I never did!" exclaimed Moira, self-righteously.

"Someone used your cell phone to call the salon," said Horowitz. "We checked the phone records."

"All right," admitted Moira. "I didn't want to lose the appointment, especially if there was going to be a funeral and everyone would be looking at me." She sniffed. "Jean-Pierre was most understanding. Very sympathetic."

"Right," said Horowitz, snapping the notebook shut. "That's all for now, but I wouldn't advise either of you to leave town. I'll need official statements, so I'll be contacting you later today or tomorrow."

Dave was on his feet immediately, heading for the door. He didn't even pause to say goodbye to Moira. She made a beeline for the elevator, with Deirdre in tow, apparently heading for the basement cafeteria.

Horowitz turned, pocketing his notebook, and spotted Lucy. "Ah, Mrs. Stone, I didn't realize you were there."

"I feel a little shaky, and I didn't want to drive until I felt better."

"You were eavesdropping."

"I didn't hear a thing," she said.

"Well, good, because then I won't have to remind you that anything you might accidentally have heard is strictly off the record. Got that?"

"Got it." Lucy stood up and crossed the room, meeting Horowitz in the middle. "I can't believe she called her hairdresser instead of nine-one-one."

"It must've been a hair emergency," said Horowitz.

Once again, Lucy's jaw dropped in amazement. "I had no idea you actually have a sense of humor," she told him.

Phyllis had the same reaction when Lucy recounted the story at the office.

Conor's exploding head. She slipped the key into the ignition, pausing when she heard the call of a seagull. It reminded her of the morning Old Dan's body was found in the harbor, and she wondered if this latest attack on Dylan was related. It seemed obvious that they must be, but why? Who was out to get the Malone brothers?

Starting the car, she was taken by a fit of yawning and realized she really was too tired to drive all the way home. Instead, she turned down Sea Street, toward the harbor, where Bill and Brian were working at the Bilge. Bill looked up in alarm when she tapped on the door.

"Is everything all right?" he asked. "Is Molly okay?"

"What have you heard?" she asked, alarmed.

"Nothing. I thought maybe you'd heard something," said Bill.

"No. Nothing from that quarter, but I do have something to tell you," said Lucy. "Somebody attacked Dylan Malone this morning. He's in the hospital, with a rock stuck in his head."

"I know he's got rocks in his head," said Brian, attempting a joke.

"No. It's true," said Lucy. "They think it came from a slingshot. He's in bad shape."

Bill sat down on a bucket of joint compound. "Damn. This could mean I'm out of a job. And you, too, Brian."

"I hadn't thought of that," admitted Brian. "I was wondering if the show's gonna go on."

"Frankly, I wouldn't mind if you never set foot in this place again," said Lucy, looking around at the big, new windows, which let in the light, and the fresh, clean wallboard. "I think you should get yourself clear of anything connected with the Malones. First, it was Old Dan, then it was Dylan, and I don't think it's a coincidence. Somebody's out to get them, and I wouldn't be surprised if the Bilge is next."

Brian and Bill exchanged glances, and Brian began to say something but was silenced by a quick shake of the head from Bill.

"Don't be silly," said Bill, giving her a hug. "You're letting your fears get the best of you."

Lucy sighed. "You're right. I'm just tired. I was heading home for a nap, but I was afraid I'd fall asleep at the wheel."

"Let's break for lunch, and I'll take you home," said Bill. "Brian, you mind picking me up in an hour or so?"

"No problem, boss," said Brian. "Meantime, I think I better make some calls. Let Frank and Father Ed know what's happened." He shrugged. "The show must go on, right?"

"That's what they say," said Lucy. "Personally, I've got some doubts."

Chapter Sixteen

Lucy went straight to bed when she got home and was awakened a little bit after three, when Sara and Zoe arrived home from school. Libby, the dog, always barked when she heard the school bus grinding its way up Red Top Hill and yipped and pranced excitedly as she awaited the wonderful moment when the door would open and the girls, who had been carried off by the big yellow monster of a school bus, would miraculously reappear. Then she would indulge in an ecstasy of wiggling, tail wagging, and jumping, which was either ignored by the girls or earned her a sharp reprimand. Today it was the latter. "Down, down, you stupid dog," ordered Sara, but Libby paid no mind. She never did until she got her treat, a handful of dog biscuits. Then she would begin hiding them, a task that kept her occupied for at least half an hour. Lucy had grown used to finding them tucked away between sofa cushions, under throw pillows and afghans, even under the pillow on her bed. That was clearly the dog's intent today. Lucy heard her nails as she clicked up the stairs and saw her slightly annoyed expression as she stood in the doorway to Lucy's room, biscuit between her teeth.

"Don't worry. I'm getting up," said Lucy. And as soon as she did, the dog jumped on her bed, dropped the biscuit, and began arranging the covers with her nose in order to hide it.

She was wondering if a dog could suffer from obsessive-compulsive behavior as she splashed some water on her face in the bathroom, then went downstairs to greet the girls. They were both sitting at the kitchen table. Zoe was eating a piece of cold pizza, and Sara was doing her homework. They both looked up when she appeared.

"How's Molly?" asked Sara.

"No news is good news, and I haven't heard anything all day," said Lucy, lighting the stove under the kettle. "I'm going to the hospital this evening."

"Can we come?" asked Sara. "I'm doing my homework right now so I can go tonight."

Lucy knew the Cottage Hospital welcomed visitors. "I don't see why not. What about you, Zoe? Do you have homework?"

"I did it at school. During reading."

Lucy nodded. This was nothing new. Zoe, who got all As, was a whiz at knocking off her homework while the kids who had trouble reading aloud made their halting way through the day's lesson. The kettle shrieked, and she made herself a cup of tea, then sat down at the table to wait for it to steep.

"Deirdre's father is in the hospital," she told Zoe. "He hurt his head."

"How did he hurt it?" asked Sara.

"Somebody threw a rock at him." Lucy pulled the tea bag out of her mug, squeezing it against the side with a spoon.

"People shouldn't throw rocks," said Zoe. "I'll make him a get well card."

"That's a good idea," said Lucy, taking a sip of tea. She felt a pleasant warming sensation in her chest, but she wasn't sure if it was the tea or Zoe's thoughtfulness that caused it.

The phone rang, and both girls stampeded across the kitchen to answer it. Sara won the race, as usual, only to learn the call wasn't for her. "It's for you, Mom," she said, sounding terribly disappointed. "It's Mrs. Goodman." Lucy wondered who she was hoping would call. A boy?

"Hi, Rachel," said Lucy, taking the phone.

"I won't keep you. I know you're busy with Molly and all," she began.

Ah, the wonders of small-town life, thought Lucy. "How'd you hear?" she asked, curious about the functioning of the gossip grapevine.

"My neighbor Susan works in the emergency room," said Rachel. "She said it was touch and go for a while there."

"Yeah," agreed Lucy. "Doc Ryder is trying to avoid a caesarean. The baby is still too small."

"That's tough. I'll be thinking of you all, especially Molly."

"I'll tell her," said Lucy. "I'm going tonight."

"Oh, that's the reason I called. To tell you Frank's calling a rehearsal at six sharp."

Lucy's eyebrows shot up. "That was fast. Dylan's in the hospital, too, you know."

"I know. Everybody's talking about it. After all, it isn't the sort of thing that happens every day. It's something straight out of *The Guinness Book of World Records.* Poor Dylan really does have rocks, or at least a rock, in his head."

Sometimes Lucy wondered why they bothered to print the *Pennysaver;* news spread so fast in this town that it hardly seemed necessary.

Getting no reply from Lucy, Rachel continued. "I know I shouldn't joke about something like this, but, well, it is pretty funny in a macabre sort of way."

Lucy started to say she didn't think it was funny at all, and that she found it extremely upsetting that somebody was running around town, chopping off heads and lob-bing rocks at people, but didn't want to say so in front of the girls. "I just hope they get to the bottom of it," she said.

"Oh, probably some kid who was messing around with a slingshot, don't you think?"

"Probably," said Lucy, who didn't think that at all. "So is Frank taking over for Dylan?"

"Just until Dylan's back on his feet. And a bit of luck for me—I'm going to take Moira's place since she'll be busy with Dylan."

"Congratulations," said Lucy, happy for her friend, even though she doubted Moira would willingly relin-quish her starring role. "I'll try to make it, but I'm not sure if I can. I want to stop at the hospital and see Molly."

"Of course. I'll explain the situation to Frank, and I'm sure he'll understand. And it's not as if you have a major role or anything. You're only in the chorus, after all."

Lucy smiled ruefully to herself. Who would have thought it? Yesterday Rachel was in the chorus; today she was a star. And already a prima donna.

After conferring with the girls, Lucy decided she would grab a quick bite at home and stop at the hospital on the way to rehearsal, and Bill and the girls would visit Molly later, after cooking supper and cleaning up the supper dishes. Lucy wasn't sure she had the energy for a rehearsal, but she knew everybody would be talking about Dylan's injury, and she didn't want to miss a word. It would be in-teresting to see how various people, especially Frank, Dave, and Brian, reacted. But first she had to assure herself that Molly was holding her own.

Toby was sitting in the recliner next to Molly's bed when Lucy arrived, watching a sports channel. Molly was sound asleep and, to Lucy's eyes, seemed to have lost some of the puffiness she'd had the day before.

"Don't get up," said Lucy as Toby started to his feet the minute he saw her. "I can't stay long."

"Should I wake Molly?" he asked, clicking off the TV.

"No, no. Let her rest." Lucy gave him a peck on the cheek. "How's she doing?"

"Okay, I guess. They won't tell me much."

"She looks better," whispered Lucy.

"Yeah. I think so, too." He looked down at his hands. "I never expected anything like this."

"It's not your fault," she told him, responding to his guilt-stricken expression. "It's not anybody's fault. It's just one of those things."

"She's never sick. She doesn't even get colds."

"Then she'll come through this just fine," said Lucy, sensing that he needed reassurance. "I'm sure of it."

"I hope so," he said, raising his voice and causing Molly to stir.

Lucy put her finger to her lip. "I guess I better go. I'm on my way to rehearsal."

"I'll walk you to the elevator," he said, getting up and casting a glance at Molly just to make sure she'd be all right in his absence. Out in the hallway, he took hold of her arm. "There's something I want to tell you, Mom," he said.

What now? Lucy turned to face him and, seeing how anxious he looked, stroked his cheek.

"There's weird stuff going on at the Bilge," he said. "It's got me kinda worried."

"What do you mean?"

"Stuff's been stolen. They've even ripped up work that Dad and Brian did. Pulled up floorboards, kicked holes in the Sheetrock, stuff like this."

"Who's doing it?" asked Lucy, alarmed.

"I think it's the old Bilge crowd. They don't like the idea of losing their hangout, you know. Now there's no place for them to go when they come off the boats."

"Do you think one of them could've thrown the rock that hit Dylan?" she asked.

"Probably. Some of those guys can be pretty crazy, especially if they're high on meth or booze or something. They wouldn't think it would really hurt him, you know?"

Lucy wasn't buying it. "Even Zoe knows you shouldn't throw rocks."

"Zoe's not using meth," said Toby. "It kinda clouds your judgment."

"And how do you know so much about it?" asked Lucy.

"Not firsthand, Mom," said Toby. "Just stuff I heard."

"Maybe you should tell some of this stuff you heard to the police. You could give Barney a call."

"That's why I'm telling you, Mom. Dad won't do anything, says it would just lead to more trouble. But I'm afraid it'll get worse if somebody doesn't stop them." He paused. "It's bad enough having Molly in the hospital. I'd hate to have Dad or Brian here, too."

"Thanks for telling me," she said, giving him a hug. "I'll see what I can do."

Then he turned and walked down the hall to Molly's room, looking as if he had the weight of the world on his shoulders.

Watching him go, Lucy shook her head sadly. He and Molly were so young, and this was a lot to handle. She sent up a little prayer for Molly and the baby and for Toby, too. Then the elevator came, and she thought over what he'd told her as she descended to the lobby and went out to the parking lot. The sun was setting, casting dazzling orange and red reflections on the hospital windows. It almost looked as if the building was on fire, but it was only a trick of the light. Soon the sun would drop below the horizon, taking all that razzle-dazzle with it and leaving darkness behind. The thought made her uneasy as she started the car. She felt vulnerable and afraid, and she didn't like it. She wanted things to go back to the way they were before Dylan and Moira came to town, bringing murder and mayhem. Oh, not that she thought they were directly responsible, but even Moira admitted they did seem to have unleashed forces that couldn't be explained or controlled.

This impression was reinforced when Lucy got to the church hall and found the rehearsal in full swing. Frank Cahill was seated at the piano, simultaneously putting the chorus members through warm-up exercises and coaching Rachel's and Dave's delivery as they ran through their lines. Brian was setting some of the finished scenery into place at the back of the stage, and it was possible to imagine what the finished set would look like. Tatiana and Fred were practicing on the front portion of the stage, where they were going through one of Og and Susan's dance numbers.

As Lucy took her place in the back row of the chorus, she could feel a real change in the atmosphere. There was a sense of purpose and positive engagement, instead of the defensiveness and backbiting that had predominated before. People were relaxed and agreeable, and to her amazement, she found her throat opening up and her voice doing what it was supposed to do as she trilled through the do-re-mi's and mama mia's, which Frank insisted upon. Beside her, Pam noticed the change and gave her a nod of approval. Then they were off and running, singing a rousing rendition of "Great Come-And-Get-It Day," which earned a big smile of approval from Frank.

"If you do it like that on opening night, we'll have a hit on our hands," said Frank. "Okay, places everyone. We're going to run through the entire show from the top."

Chorus members arranged themselves on stage as Frank played the overture. Then he gave the signal, and they began singing "This Time of the Year," which was fol-

lowed by Susan's dance number. Then Rachel made her
entrance as Sharon, singing her big song, the haunting
"How Are Things In Glocca Morra?"

The song was meant to evoke the Irish countryside and
to express Sharon's longing for her homeland when she
found herself in rural Missitucky, accompanying her father, Finian, who had a fantastic scheme to become
wealthy. Until now, Lucy had never heard the entire song,
because Moira had always found some self-serving reason
to interrupt it before she had to hit the high notes. She'd
stamp her foot and demand silence; she'd claim Frank was
playing in the wrong key; she'd have to pause and spray
her throat. Rachel, however, didn't indulge in any of these
tricks. She simply sang the song in a pure, clear voice that
brought the beautiful images of springtime in Ireland to
life. When she ended, the chorus spontaneously burst into
applause. Lucy's and Pam's eyes met. Realizing that they
were both blinking back tears, they laughed and hugged
each other.

"Bravo!" exclaimed Frank.

Rachel, her face scarlet, shifted uncomfortably from one
foot to another. "I wasn't that good," she protested. "Especially that part . . ."

"Nonsense. You are a breath of fresh air, my dear,"
replied Frank. "It's as if you transported us all to the auld
sod. But enough. We have work to do." He pounded a few
chords, everyone shuffled back in place, and Rachel
segued into "Look to the Rainbow."

Again, Rachel was right on target, delivering a flawless
performance. The chorus also managed, for the first time,
to come in on cue and on key. What had been a confusing
muddle with innumerable distractions and annoying
stops and starts now began to make sense. It was working, and everybody was caught up in the momentum,
thoroughly engaged and enjoying it. All their hard work

suddenly seemed to be paying off in this glorious, magical moment.

The mood was shattered when Moira appeared, announcing her arrival by throwing open the door so hard that it banged against the wall. "What the hell's going on here?" she demanded, striding through the folding chairs that were scattered about the hall and mounting the center steps to the stage, where she turned and leaned over, glaring down at Frank and shaking a finger at him. "You're responsible for this! You couldn't wait to replace me with this . . . this . . . amateur!"

Frank stood up. "First of all, you're late, Moira. Just like you've been late for every rehearsal. Second, since I didn't hear a word from you to the contrary, I assumed you would want to be at your husband's bedside. And thirdly," he continued, warming to his theme, "you stink. You can't sing; you won't learn your lines; you're a pain in the butt. And since I'm directing, I've decided to get rid of you and give your part to Rachel."

"Who says you're directing?" asked Moira, archly. "I don't believe my husband, the *director*, has resigned. He's under contract, you know, and accor—"

Frank was definitely losing altitude. "Be reasonable, Moira. The man is in the hospital, he can't possibly . . ."

"As I was saying before I was so rudely interrupted, there is a clause in the contract that covers exactly this contingency. If he is unable to direct, I will take his place, consulting with him frequently and relying on his excellent *professional* advice."

"But I heard he was unconscious," protested Frank.

"He is expected to regain consciousness shortly, and besides, I know him so well that I can divine his thoughts."

At this, Frank simply sat down on the piano bench and buried his face in his arms.

"I will carry out my husband's wishes," declared Moira,

flipping open her script. "I will direct *and* play the role of Sharon."

There was a stunned silence as Rachel simply nodded her assent and stepped aside. Lucy searched her friend's face for any sign of emotion, but Rachel's eyes remained dry, and her expression was neutral, except for a fluttering little vein in her temple. Moira ignored her, furiously turning the pages of the script, finally finding her place. "Let's continue. Where's Woody? Woody?"

Dave Reilly emerged from backstage, where he'd withdrawn when Moira arrived. Lucy certainly didn't blame him, after the scene in the hospital, but Moira behaved as if nothing had happened.

"There you are!" exclaimed Moira, slipping her arm through his. "Maestro!" She pointed at Frank. "Are you ready?"

Frank nodded glumly.

Moira waved her arm at the chorus. "Off with you, now. This is Woody's and my big love song." She was still hanging on to his arm, but poor Dave looked at her warily, as if she might lose her temper any minute.

But Moira was all pats and smiles. "We don't need them, do we?" she cooed.

The chorus shuffled off, making a good deal of noise as they settled themselves on chairs and opened newspapers and began chatting to each other. When Rachel didn't appear, Pam went to look for her in the ladies' room, while Lucy perched nervously on a chair. Frank played the first few bars of the song, but Moira waved her arms, calling for silence.

"This is intolerable!" she shrieked. "How am I supposed to perform under these conditions?"

"I dunno, sweetheart," muttered Frank. "Why don't you ask that husband of yours? THE DIRECTOR!"

At this, Moira threw herself on poor Dave Reilly, burying her face in his chest and sobbing loudly. It was then that Rachel reappeared, accompanied by Pam, and slipped into the chair next to Lucy's. "Here we go, again," she said, her voice quavering slightly.

"Are you okay?" whispered Lucy.

"I'm better than okay," said Rachel, her eyes blazing. "And on my worst day, I'm better than that Moira!"

Chapter Seventeen

With Molly in the hospital, time seemed to drag for Lucy. She wanted the clock to speed up and the days to fly by until it was time for Molly to deliver a healthy baby. But instead, they seemed to stretch out interminably, and if it was like that for her, she could only imagine what poor Molly was going through. Lucy had plenty to do every day, both at work and at home. She was out and about, talking to people, conducting interviews, covering meetings, writing stories, and then, when she was done at the paper, she was shopping at the grocery store, preparing meals, doing laundry, keeping tabs on the girls, walking the dog, talking to friends on the phone, and busy with all the little matters of everyday life. And, of course, there were the rehearsals for *Finian's Rainbow*. With Dylan out of the picture, in the hospital, the rehearsals would have proceeded smoothly under Frank's direction, but Moira's increasingly frequent emotional outbursts drained everyone's patience.

For Molly, there was nothing to do but lie in the hospital and wait and hope that everything was going to be all right. So far, things had gone well, and that was a blessing. But there was always that sense of life suspended, of waiting, and it was driving Lucy crazy.

Even Wednesday, deadline day, which was usually a

frantic scramble to get the week's copy to the printer, seemed unusually quiet this week. Lucy and Phyllis had finished the events listings with time to spare, and the police and fire logs were ready. Lucy had even finished the feature story about the metal prospectors, which Ted was running with her photo of the 1776 coin. All that was missing was Ted's update on the Dylan Malone story, which he would write when he got back from yet another press conference at the police station.

"Are you sure we haven't forgotten something?" asked Phyllis, taking a bottle of nail polish out of her desk drawer and shaking it.

"Nope," said Lucy, shaking her head. "I've checked and double-checked the news budget, and we are good. Is that a new color?"

"Kelly green. I thought I'd get in the spirit for St. Patrick's Day. I've got a green sweater with little shamrocks, a pair of green slacks, even green shoes."

"You don't think it's too much green?"

"Not for St. Pat's Day."

"But you're not even Irish."

"Everybody's Irish on St. Patrick's Day. Elfrida's cooking up a corned beef and cabbage dinner—she asked me to make Irish soda bread, but I'm only going to have a teeny slice—and then we're all going to the show. I bought the tickets Sunday, after church."

"Since when do you go to church on Sunday?"

"Ever since I started seeing Bobby Monahan."

"I didn't know you had a gentleman friend."

"I met him at the gym," replied Phyllis, looking smug. "We were both doing the Atkins diet."

"And is he coming to this family dinner?"

"You betcha. Wouldn't miss it for the world, he says, though I warned him Elfrida's cooking can be a bit unusual."

"How so?"

"She's been experimenting with food coloring. At Christmas, everything was either red or green, and I'm pretty sure the whole meal will be green for St. Patrick's Day."

"That's no big deal. There's green beer, green mashed potatoes, green jello, green salad, green cabbage. . . ."

"Green corned beef," said Phyllis.

"Oh," said Lucy, looking up as Ted came in, seeming rather flustered. "Did you run the whole way?" she asked him.

"You bet I did," he said, panting as he took off his coat and tossed it at the hall stand. It usually caught on the hook, but this time it missed and fell to the floor in a crumpled heap, but Ted was too excited to notice. "You are not going to believe this."

Lucy was doubtful. She'd been to too many police press conferences that were a waste of time. "Believe what?"

"What I'm going to tell you, but first, I've gotta warn you it's kind of icky," said Ted.

Lucy and Phyllis looked at each other. "I think we can handle it, Ted," said Lucy. "I'm a mother, and Phyllis eats Elfrida's cooking. Between the two of us, we've pretty much seen it all."

"Trust me, this is weird," replied Ted.

"We're sitting down, Ted. Tell us, for goodness sake," snapped Phyllis.

"Okay," said Ted. "They finally got the report, the analysis, of the rock in Dylan's head, and it wasn't a rock at all."

"A marble egg?" guessed Phyllis. "I always thought those things were dangerous."

"Not a marble egg. It was a . . ." He paused.

"A what?" demanded Lucy.

"A petrified brain. A human brain," said Ted.

"I think I'm going to be sick," said Phyllis, whose face matched her Kelly green nails.

"Yuck," said Lucy. "You weren't kidding. Talk about icky."

Phyllis was on her feet, hurrying to the bathroom.

"I tried to warn her," said Ted. "Are you okay with this?"

"Like I said, I'm a mother. You name it, I've seen it and probably had to mop it up," said Lucy. She thought for a minute. "I thought brains were kind of squishy."

"Normally, they are," agreed Ted, clearly fascinated by the story, "but this was a mummified brain. It was mixed with lime and shaped into a ball. See, here's the picture they gave us."

Lucy looked at the photo of a small gray lump. "Is this a whole brain or just part?" she asked as Phyllis emerged from the bathroom. "I mean, I don't see how you could mash a whole brain into something this compact."

"Bluuegh," moaned Phyllis, grabbing her stomach and heading straight back to the bathroom.

"I was wondering about that, too," said Ted, sitting down in his chair and booting up his computer in preparation to write the story. "They're not actually sure if it's an entire brain or not, but they know for sure that it is cerebral matter."

"I suppose a lot of brain tissue is actually water," said Lucy as Phyllis poked her head out from behind the bathroom door.

"Are you still talking about you know what?" asked Phyllis.

"Not if it upsets you," said Lucy. "I'll just read Ted's story over his shoulder."

"No, it's okay," said Phyllis. "I had an idea while I was in there. About the you know what."

"What was your idea?" asked Ted.

"Well, I was wondering where a person would get, well, you know what, and then I remembered Old Dan and how

ST. PATRICK'S DAY MURDER   193

his head was missing," said Phyllis. "Maybe that's where the you know what came from."

"They thought of that. They're doing DNA testing to see if it matches," said Ted.

"The police think that Dylan was hit with his own brother's . . . ," began Lucy, pausing as she saw Phyllis's expression.

"That's what they think," said Ted.

"Somebody must really hate them both, both Malone brothers," said Lucy. "Like it's some sort of family feud. Maybe something going way back, even. Remember I told you about Celtic warriors making brain balls?"

"The cops are looking for an Irish connection," said Ted, typing away on his keyboard. "They're contacting Irish officials, but so far Dylan doesn't seem to have any gangland or IRA connections. No record at all. Ditto for Old Dan."

He looked up. "It's half past eleven," he said. "A half hour to deadline, and I don't see the town meeting warrant."

Lucy looked vacant. "Town meeting warrant?"

"It came Monday," replied Ted.

"I wasn't here Monday, remember?" said Lucy.

"Well, I need an overview, an explanation for voters of what's important," said Ted. "Like the five hundred thousand dollars for open space."

"But I haven't even read it," said Lucy, who was frantically searching through the messy pile of papers on her desk. "Much less interviewed the selectmen."

"You've got thirty minutes," said Ted just as Lucy found the warrant tucked inside a brochure from the senior center, announcing April activities, that Lucy was saving to use for a story next week.

She groaned, flipping through the closely printed pages. "But there's twenty-nine pages packed with one hundred thirty-four articles. . . ."

"Thirty minutes."

* * *

It was a struggle, and she felt more like a sprinter than a writer, but Lucy managed to condense the town meeting warrant into eighteen inches of copy, including a quote from the chairman of the board of selectmen about how important it was for voters to attend town meetings and to approve the entire warrant, especially a spending article calling for that half-million-dollar open space purchase.

"Good work, Lucy," said Ted, giving her a rare nod of approval. "Now get out of here."

"See you tomorrow," said Phyllis, with a wave of her green-tipped hand.

Out on the sidewalk, Lucy buttoned up her coat against the chilly March wind and decided to air out her brain and work out a few muscle kinks by walking the few blocks to Miss Tilley's house, where she was expected for lunch. As she passed the stores lining Main Street, she noticed that many of them had decorated their windows with green paper cutouts of shamrocks and leprechauns. The library had a sign announcing a St. Patrick's Day tea, and there was a colorful sandwich board on the church lawn, complete with a rainbow and the dancing figures of Sharon and Finian announcing the show. Lucy counted the days until opening night and discovered it was in a little more than two weeks.

They were going to need a miracle, she thought, rounding the corner onto Miss Tilley's street. A blast of wind blowing off the cove nearly knocked her off her feet and snatched her breath away, but it wasn't the razor-sharp blast of cold that she'd grown to expect in the last few months. Spring was really on its way, she decided, spotting a clump of lavender crocus that had sprouted in the shelter of a rock. Another blast of wind reminded her that spring came very slowly in Maine, beginning with mud season and ending with the emergence of swarms of black flies, but in between there was always a handful of precious balmy days, when the grass suddenly turned green, vibrant emerald leaves erupted from gray tree bark, and the lilacs and apple trees bloomed, scenting the air.

Lucy vowed to keep that thought as she struggled against the wind, grabbing hold of the railing to haul herself onto Miss Tilley's stoop. When she opened the storm door, she had to struggle to keep the wind from taking it and slamming it against the railing while she knocked and waited for Rachel to open the front door.

"Look what the wind blew in," exclaimed Rachel when Lucy stepped inside the little Cape Cod–style cottage. A glance at the hall mirror showed her the wind had tugged her hair out from under her hat, had tangled her scarf, and had reddened her cheeks. No matter. Lucy went straight to Miss Tilley, who was sitting in her usual place, in the rocker next to the fireplace. It was too windy for a fire, but Rachel had placed a little heater on the hearth, and Miss Tilley's hands were warm when Lucy grasped them.

"She's brought the cold with her," complained Miss Tilley. "You should feel her hands. They're like ice."

"You're nice and cozy in here," said Lucy, taking the opposite chair.

"Give her some of Papa's brandy. That'll warm her up," said Miss Tilley.

Puzzled, Lucy glanced at Rachel, who responded with a shrug. "We don't have any brandy, only sherry," said Rachel, handing Lucy a glass.

"Well, you better get some brandy," said Miss Tilley. "Papa has to have his brandy."

"Not a good day," mouthed Rachel, retreating behind Miss Tilley's chair. "I'll have lunch ready in a minute," she said out loud, then retreated to the kitchen.

True to her word, they were soon seated at the antique cherry drop-leaf dining table, where a copper lusterware pitcher held a bouquet of supermarket daffodils, and Rachel dished out helpings of Irish stew.

"This is delicious," said Lucy, tucking right in.

"Be sure to save some for Papa," said Miss Tilley. "It's one of his favorite dishes."

"Don't worry. There's plenty for Papa, too," said Rachel.

Lucy was surprised that she didn't attempt to reorient the old woman in the present by reminding her that her father had been dead for nearly fifty years.

"He can have his later," continued Rachel, watching anxiously as Miss Tilley slowly picked up her fork and began to eat. Turning to Lucy, she said, "Miss T hasn't had much appetite lately."

"I just want to make sure there's something left for Papa," said Miss Tilley, clearly lost in the past.

"There's enough for everyone," said Rachel. "There's a big pot of stew in the kitchen, so eat as much as you like."

"It is very tasty," admitted Miss Tilley. "But not quite as good as Brigid's. Papa likes Brigid's Irish stew, but she's not here anymore." She leaned across the table and put her hand on Lucy's arm, ready to share a choice bit of gossip. "She went to the ambassador's house, and I hear there's mischief afoot up there."

After getting a nod from Rachel, Lucy decided to play along. "Really? What sort of mischief?"

"All sorts," replied Miss Tilley. "There's no woman in the house, you see, except for Brigid, since Mrs. O'Donnell died of cancer." She clucked her tongue. "They say she suffered terribly all alone there, with the ambassador away so much and the boys too busy with Brigid to pay her any mind."

"I didn't realize the O'Donnell boys lost their mother," said Lucy. "Maybe that explains why Mikey Boy turned to crime."

"Cormac's no better," insisted Miss Tilley, as if she were sharing something scandalous. "He's a Democrat, you know."

"Being a Democrat isn't quite the same as being a gangster," protested Rachel.

"It's worse," said Miss Tilley, prompting both Lucy and Rachel to laugh.

"You can laugh," chided Miss Tilley, "but you'll see. Nixon's going to beat that Kennedy boy."

Lucy smiled at this, but when she glanced at Rachel, she noticed she was brushing away a tear. She felt a surge of sympathy for her friend. She had been caring for Miss Tilley for years, stopping by casually with a plate of food or a bunch of flowers after the old woman was involved in a tragic automobile accident and gradually taking on more and more responsibility. Now she even got paid, after a social worker from Elder Services visited and decided she qualified as a home health aide. Rachel had never viewed caring for Miss Tilley as a job; she was simply helping a friend. And now she must be terribly worried that she was losing that friend.

Lucy decided it was time to change the subject. "Are you coming to the show?" she asked. "I'm in the chorus, and Rachel has a real part."

"A small part," said Rachel, smiling wryly.

"I've heard her practicing the songs," said Miss Tilley. "She has a beautiful voice."

"I know," said Lucy. "She's the understudy for the star, so maybe—"

"No chance of that," said Rachel, beginning to clear the table. "I have no doubt that if Moira were dead and buried, she would rise from the grave to take the stage."

"Like Mikey Boy," said Miss Tilley, smacking her lips when Rachel set a dish of ice cream in front of her.

"Mikey Boy died?" asked Lucy.

The old woman popped a spoonful of ice cream into her mouth, and another, before she answered. "They said he did when they were going to put him on trial for murdering an FBI man. They had a funeral and everything, but then it turned out, he wasn't dead at all. He went into hiding, and he's been hiding ever since, but sometimes you see pictures of him in the paper, in Spain and places like that."

"The family had a funeral?" asked Lucy, wondering how accurate the old woman's information could be.

Miss Tilley nodded, scraping her bowl and licking the spoon. "I hope there's ice cream for Papa, too. He loves ice cream."

When she left, Lucy felt her mind was in just as much turmoil as the weather. The wind was picking up dry leaves and old candy wrappers and whirling them around, much like the fragmentary ideas she couldn't seem to grasp. She knew Cormac O'Donnell was the good brother, the public servant everyone admired. And she knew he had a brother who everyone considered evil, a sort of bad seed, who had also risen to prominence in organized crime and made the FBI's Ten Most Wanted list. But she had always understood that the O'Donnell family, and Cormac particularly, had made every effort to distance themselves from Mikey Boy. In fact, she clearly remembered reading quite recently in the *Boston Globe* that Cormac had appeared before a grand jury and been questioned about his brother but had maintained there had been no contact for many years.

Well, maybe it was true, she thought, fighting against the wind at the corner of Main Street. But if what Miss Tilley had told her about a fake funeral was true, it certainly seemed there had been some sort of family collusion in Mikey Boy's flight from this country to Europe. Maybe Miss Tilley was on to something. Maybe there wasn't that much difference between organized crime and politics, at least in the O'Donnell family. Maybe the brothers weren't that different, after all.

By the time she had struggled a couple of blocks down

Main Street, fighting the wind every step of the way, Lucy was looking for shelter. Pausing for a moment in the lee of a big old tree, she noticed she was in front of the police station. It occurred to her that Barney might be there, and he might have heard something about the O'Donnell brothers. It was worth asking—even if it only got her out of the wind for a few minutes.

But when she battled her way inside, forcing the door open against the wind and then hanging on to it with all her strength when the wind caught it, she forgot all about Barney and the O'Donnell brothers. Her attention was immediately caught by Moira, whose hysterical screams rang against the concrete walls and bounced off the reinforced steel doors and even seemed to rattle the bulletproof Plexiglas protecting the officer on reception duty.

He tried several times to ask what was the matter, but Moira ignored him, throwing her head back and tossing her wild red hair and beating on the Plexiglas barrier with her fists. Finally, he came through the steel door and grabbed her by her elbows.

"Lady, you've got to calm down and tell me what's the problem. Okay?"

At his touch, Moira seemed to subside, withdrawing inside her black cloak. Then, slowly, with exquisite grace, two white hands emerged from its folds and grasped the officer's navy blue shirt. "You have to help me," she said between sobs. "My Deirdre's disappeared!"

Chapter Eighteen

"Lady, how the hell am I supposed to know who Deirdre is?" asked the officer. "Is it your cat? Dog? When did you last see him?"

"Her," said Lucy, answering for Moira, who had seized her with both hands and was hanging on to her for support and sobbing into her shoulder. "Deirdre is her daughter. She's nine years old."

The officer looked at them suspiciously. "Say, you look familiar. Weren't you in here a couple of weeks ago with some missing kids?"

"That was a misunderstanding," admitted Lucy, who was convinced Moira was telling the truth. Her whole body was shaking, and she was crying real, wet tears, which were staining Lucy's new winter coat with fur trim, which she'd bought last month at an end-of-season sale.

The officer wasn't convinced. "Lady, do you know what it does to the tax rate every time we have one of these false alarms?"

Lucy knew only too well. Last summer she'd written about an extensive search for two hikers who had wandered off the Adirondack Trail, right into a cozy—and secluded—B and B. But there was no denying the drama queen was genuinely upset, so upset that her mascara was running in ugly black streaks down her face.

The steel door leading to the offices beyond opened, and Lucy was relieved when Barney Culpepper came into the waiting room. "What's going on?" he asked.

"Deirdre Malone is missing," said Lucy.

"Again?" asked Barney, incredulously.

"No," snapped Lucy. "For the first time." Moira was a slight woman, but even so, her weight was beginning to be more than Lucy could manage. She led her to the row of battered plastic chairs set against the wall and sat her down, taking the seat beside her.

"I know you're upset," she said, stroking Moira's curly hair. "But you have to tell us what happened. The police need as much information as you can give them." She took hold of both of Moira's hands and looked her in the eye. "Can you help us?"

Barney and the desk officer shared a glance.

Moira sniffed—it was really more of a snort, providing yet more proof that she was genuinely distressed—and took a deep breath. "She had a playdate, and Sadie's mother was supposed to drop her off at the house at one. I was running late. I got there at a quarter past, and there was no sign of her. At first, I assumed Sadie's mom was also running late, and I was relieved. But when there was no sign of them after fifteen minutes or so, I gave her a call. She said she'd dropped Deirdre at the house at five past."

Now Lucy was beginning to have some doubts. "Juanita Orenstein wouldn't do that. She wouldn't leave a child she was caring for in an empty house."

"She said she didn't want to do it, but she was running late and Sadie had a doctor's appointment and Deirdre had insisted it would be all right." She looked at Lucy with enormous eyes. "She's gone. There was no sign she'd even been in the house. No coat, no shoes. Nothing."

Lucy didn't like the sound of this at all, especially considering what had happened to Old Dan and Dylan, but the officers remained skeptical, even Barney.

"Mebbe you better get an incident report form," Barney told the desk officer. He raised an eyebrow meaningfully. "CYA, if you know what I mean."

When the desk officer returned with a clipboard and began questioning Moira, Lucy took Barney aside. "Something's going on," she told him. "Somebody's out to get the Malones. First it was Old Dan, then it was Dylan, and now it's Deirdre. It's a blood feud. There's no other explanation."

Barney looked doubtful. "Like the Hatfields and the McCoys?"

"Something like that," said Lucy as a suspicion blossomed in her mind. She turned to Moira. "Who was your husband's mother? What was her name? Her maiden name?"

"What on earth does that have to do with this?" demanded Moira.

"Possibly everything. Who was she?" said Lucy.

"Her name was Brigid, Brigid Heaney," replied Moira.

Lucy felt as if she'd put the last piece in a jigsaw puzzle. Suddenly, everything made sense. "I knew it," she said. "It's not the Hatfields and McCoys. It's the Malones and the O'Donnells. They go way back. Miss Tilley told me that Brigid Heaney, Old Dan and Dylan's mother, worked for the O'Donnells years ago, until she left in a hurry and went back to Ireland and married her old boyfriend. A child, probably Old Dan, was born soon after."

"Hold on, Lucy," protested Barney. "You're jumping to conclusions here. Think about it. Do you really think that Cormac O'Donnell would risk his future in politics to get even with . . . who? A maid or cook or somebody who hasn't been seen or heard from for years and years?"

Lucy had to admit it was a bit of a stretch. But then she remembered Cormac wasn't the only O'Donnell brother. "Not Cormac," she said, slowly. "It must be Mikey Boy."

Barney shook his head, and his jowls quivered. "No way. He's gone. He's been out of the country for years."

"That's what everybody thinks, but nobody actually knows his whereabouts. He could've come back, slipped in from Canada or something. Think about it. Remember that FBI guy that Mikey Boy killed. His body was mutilated, wasn't it?"

"No head or hands," admitted Barney. "Typical gangland stuff so the body couldn't be identified."

"Maybe," said Lucy. "But I did some research on that brain ball thing, and I found that ancient Celtic warriors used to make them and carry them around for bragging rights."

Barney looked at her as if she were crazy. "I've heard you come up with some pretty crazy ideas, Lucy, but this takes the cake. You think Mikey Boy has come home like some sort of Celtic warrior to avenge an old wrong? He's risking his freedom, maybe even his life, to wipe out the Malones?"

Moira, who had finished answering the desk officer's questions, suddenly spoke up. "And he's doing a fine job of it, too."

Barney's head snapped around. "Do you think it's Mikey Boy?"

"I have no idea," said Moira. "I never heard of him 'til the other day. But somebody is out to get us, and it's somebody who knows the old Irish tales."

"Moira," said Lucy, taking the woman's hands in her own, "can you think of anyone who wants to harm your family?"

"On the contrary," she said, lifting her chin up proudly. "We are the darlings of Irish theater. I thought everyone loved us."

Barney shook his head and grabbed the incident report, which he quickly scanned, then told the desk officer to take it to the captain. He was soon back. "Captain wants to see you," said the desk officer, pointing at Moira. When

Lucy got up, too, he shook his head. "Just her," he said, ushering Moira through the door.

Lucy looked at Barney. "What's going on?"

"Captain wants to be sure before he calls the state police and requests another AMBER Alert."

"Will he do it?"

"I don't think he's got any choice. The mother says her kid is missing, and it seems more'n likely she was abducted, probably snatched before she even set foot in the house. The crime-scene guys will go over the house. We'll know more then." He sighed. "You don't s'pose she coulda wandered off on her own?"

"She's an imaginative little thing and believes in fairies and all sorts of magical creatures, but it doesn't seem likely. She's not an outdoorsy kid, and it's awfully cold today. And it still gets dark pretty early this time of year," said Lucy, who was feeling guilty for forbidding Zoe to play with Deirdre. If she'd been at their house, this might never have happened. "She's pretty self-sufficient. I have a feeling she's used to spending a lot of time by herself. I think she would have gone into the house and made herself comfortable with a book until her mother got home."

The door opened, and the desk officer was back with orders for Barney. "Captain wants you to take a look-see at the house. It's on Bumps River Road."

"I know where it is," said Barney, following him through the door and leaving Lucy alone in the waiting room.

She sat for a few minutes, trying to decide what to do. Her first impulse was to stay put. She didn't want to abandon Moira, who might need emotional support, or just a ride home. But as she sat in the empty room, listening to the tick of the big clock on the wall as the minute hand lurched its way through the hour, she began to have second thoughts. She knew how the police operated, and she was pretty sure Moira was undergoing some pretty intensive questioning by investigators following strict procedures. They would insist on questioning Moira alone; they wouldn't want a companion confusing the issue. And if Moira needed a ride home, they had plenty of cars.

In fact, she realized as she left the building, there were signs that the captain was taking Deirdre's disappearance very seriously. She could see through the window that the parking lot beside the station was filling up with official vehicles, including several from the state police and neighboring towns. And when she got in her car and started it, the AMBER Alert was announced on the radio.

Just hearing the description of Deirdre as "a nine-year-old, with freckles, wearing a pink parka and white snow boots" made Lucy feel as if a tight hand was squeezing her heart. Too often she'd read about innocent little girls who got into cars with neighbors or strangers, uncles or family friends, who promised them ice cream and treats but instead gave them something they'd never expected. After using them up, they threw the little girls' broken bodies away in the woods or along a deserted road, like so much trash. And if Deirdre was in Mikey Boy's clutches, there was no limit to what he might do.

When the white crime-scene van arrived, Lucy came to a decision. The van would go to the Malone house, which would be the focus of the investigation. But she had a different idea. There was another house she thought deserved a closer look: the O'Donnell place on Shore Road.

From the outside, the big, old Shingle-style mansion looked deserted. There were no cars in the white oyster-shell drive. There was no comfortable wicker furniture scattered on the big porches, no beach towels were drying on the railings, and no white muslin curtains flapped at the tightly closed and shuttered windows that looked blindly out toward the sea. All seemed closed up tight against the winter weather as Lucy walked around the house, looking for signs of habitation. There was nothing, nothing at all. Even the plastic garbage cans by the kitchen door were empty, Each one weighted by a single cement block.

It was when she was replacing the lid on the last one that she noticed a small, square door, probably originally designed for coal or ice deliveries when the house was built in the late eighteen hundreds. There was no reason why anyone would use it nowadays, but the winter brown grass in front of it had been worn away, down to bare earth. She stood, staring at it, trying to think of some explanation. An animal? No, the door was secured with a ring and hasp fastened by a padlock. As she stooped down to take a closer look, she remembered the words of the old prospector she'd encountered in the cemetery at Old Dan's funeral. He'd recited an old Irish curse: "May the grass grow before your door." She was thinking about this when a sudden caw made her jump. Looking up to the sky, she saw a flock of crows winging by, calling to each other. They flapped on, and she bent down again to examine the lock. It had the fuzzy, dull look that galvanized metal acquires when it is exposed to the elements, except for the area around the keyhole, which had bright and shiny scratch marks. Somebody had been using that door quite recently, somebody who didn't want to make his presence known.

Lucy dropped the lock as if it were burning her hand and ran back to her car as quickly as she could. She didn't think that Mikey Boy, and that's exactly who she suspected it was, would appreciate her company, so she started the car and drove as quickly as she could down the drive. Once she was on Shore Road, deserted this time of year, she called the police station and asked to speak to Barney. Much to her surprise, she was put through.

"I thought you'd be out at the Malone house," she said.

"Just got back."

"Did you find anything?"

"Nope. Tire tracks, but they match Moira's car."

"I think I may have found something." She took a deep breath. "Somebody's been coming and going at the O'Donnell house."

"I don't think so, Lucy. We do regular patrols on Shore Road. I do 'em myself sometimes. There's nobody out there this time of year except raccoons and crows."

"Well, this raccoon can use a lock and key," said Lucy, braking at the stop sign. "I think you ought to take a look inside the house."

"Gosh, Lucy, you know I can't do that without a warrant, and with all this AMBER Alert going on, how do you think I'm going to get the captain to call the judge? Huh?"

Lucy knew he was right. The department wasn't equipped to handle much more than traffic stops and petty crimes. "Well, can you come and take a look at the lock? From the outside?"

"Yeah, I'm due for a break. Meet me at the Quik Stop."

Lucy had an enormous cup of coffee with cream and eight sugars and a bag of donuts ready for Barney when he pulled alongside her in the cruiser. She hopped into the passenger seat, and he swung out of the parking lot in that confident way cops have, not seeming to check if anybody's coming. He made short work of the donuts and coffee as he sped down the road, with his lights flashing. Minutes later they were both crouched down by the door, studying the lock and examining the ground.

"You're right, Lucy," he said, finally, as he straightened up. "Somebody's been living here." He nodded toward a small cellar window. "See that? The window's been covered with cardboard so the light won't show."

Lucy hadn't noticed it before, but Barney was right. She listened as he pulled out his radio and reported their findings to the station in an unemotional, businesslike tone. It wasn't until he clicked off that he allowed his emotions to show.

"Whew," he said, his eyes bright with excitement. "This is something. I mean, if Mikey Boy is really back and I, I mean we, discover him and they actually capture him, well, you know. Wow!"

"It would be quite a scoop," said Lucy, picturing herself receiving first place for investigative reporting at the New England Newspaper Association convention.

"Yeah," agreed Barney, imagining himself on *Inside Edition*, chatting with Deborah Norville.

Their daydreams were interrupted by the arrival of the crime-scene van. "So whatcha got?" demanded the head technician.

"This house is supposed to be deserted, but somebody's been using it," said Barney, leading him to the door.

"Whose house is it?" asked the technician, quickly surveying the situation.

"The lieutenant governor's," said Barney.

The tech's eyebrows shot up. "Cormac O'Donnell? Say, isn't his brother wanted by the FBI?"

"He's the one," said Barney.

The tech gave a low whistle, then crouched by the door and lifted the lock with a pencil to examine it. He straightened up slowly, examining the ground in front of the door, and Lucy found herself holding her breath. What if they were wrong? What if all they'd done was start a big goose chase? "Cameras," said the tech. "I need pictures. We've definitely got signs of entry by somebody who doesn't want to use the front door."

Lucy had never seen anything like it. The sun had set, briefly tinting the sky a blazing shade between pink and orange, but it was as light as day outside the O'Donnell place, thanks to bright lights set up by police investigators.

The entire state police force seemed to be on the scene, along with local cops from Tinker's Cove and nearby towns, and a handful of FBI and ATF investigators, identifiable by the white initials on their black Windbreakers. The news of a possible Mikey Boy capture had spread fast, and several network TV trucks were parked on Shore Road, with their satellite dishes thrust high into the sky on collapsible poles.

The investigators were concentrating on the cellar, where it was clear that Mikey Boy had taken up residence. He'd made himself quite comfortable with a cot and sleeping bag. He had a fancy radio that picked up international stations and had even rigged up cable TV.

"I don't think he went to all this trouble to watch *American Idol*, said one agent, lugging out the TV.

"Nah," agreed another, who was carrying the tagged radio. "A fugitive's gotta keep up with the news."

The agents were systematically stripping the cellar, carrying away everything as evidence, right down to the boxes of groceries. They were also looking for a hidey-hole or escape hatch, but Lucy gathered from their conversation that they weren't having much success. "They sure don't build 'em like this anymore," said one cop, emerging from the cellar, with cobwebs and dust clinging to his white jumpsuit. "Those cellar walls are solid rock, three feet thick."

"Well, it's all yours," said another, who was carrying a box of assorted items, which he added to the collection set on the lawn. "This is the last of the stuff."

Another technician, who was logging the items as evidence before stowing them in a van, nodded.

Curious, Lucy approached and started checking out the stuff. It would make a good human interest angle. What sort of stuff did Mikey Boy have in his hidey-hole?

A lot of peanut butter, she discovered, and plenty of toilet paper. He apparently had a sweet tooth, judging from the large amount of candy, with a special fondness for Butter-finger bars. There were a couple of bottles of Jameson, too, but they hadn't been opened. There were plenty of warm clothes and boots, a pair of high-powered binoculars, and in the same box, a metal detector.

Lucy stared at it so long that the technician noticed. "It's a metal detector," he told her. "Mebbe he was look-ing for some loot he'd buried years ago. They never did turn up that two million from the armored truck job."

"I know what it is," said Lucy, with a smile. And, sud-denly, she also knew who Mikey Boy was. She'd even spo-ken to him and asked if she could take his picture. No wonder he'd refused. She hurried off, looking for someone to tell. Someone in authority who'd believe her, like Detec-tive Horowitz. She spotted him walking toward his car, followed by a clutch of reporters with microphones.

"No comment," he was saying as he opened the door.

The reporters peppered him with questions. "Are you sure it's Mikey Boy? How do you know? Has he abducted the girl? How did he get in the country? Do you think he's still around?"

Horowitz brushed them all off. "As soon as we have anything definite, we'll make a statement," he said, seating himself behind the steering wheel.

"Detective!" screamed Lucy, over the others. "I have something I have to tell you."

He either didn't hear or ignored her, and slammed the door shut, then slowly drove off.

"Damn!" she muttered, stamping her foot.

"You can say that again," agreed a photographer, studying the display on his digital camera. "This light's impossible."

Lucy stared at him, speechless. Didn't he realize there was more at stake here than getting a good picture? All the excitement about Michael O'Donnell's return had distracted everyone's attention from the missing girl. If Mikey Boy was carrying out an ancient vendetta against the Malones and had abducted little Deirdre, the child was in grave danger, and every second counted.

Chapter Nineteen

Lucy was furious as she watched Horowitz drive away. She was sure she could identify Mikey Boy; she even had the fake name he was using: Paul Sullivan. She could certainly describe him, too: late sixties, thinning hair, average height, average weight, clean-shaven. Come to think of it, maybe her description wouldn't be all that helpful. It was no wonder Mikey Boy had eluded capture all these years—he was so average looking, he blended in. His description fit thousands, probably millions, of men. He could sit down at a town meeting, for example, and would be indistinguishable from dozens of worthy citizens in their plaid shirts and khaki pants.

There was one way he was different from them, however. If what she'd read and heard about him was true, he was completely without a conscience. He lied and stole and cheated—and killed—without remorse.

This was a man who hadn't quailed at beheading one victim and using the victim's compacted brain in an attempt to murder another. Her mind balked when she tried to imagine what he had in mind for little Deirdre, but the very thought that the little girl was in his snare horrified her. Nothing was more important than finding them and rescuing the child.

The thought energized her, and she hurried to her car,

determined to find Deirdre. But where? The police didn't seem to be having any luck searching the O'Donnell house. And even if there was some sort of hidey-hole there, it would take them all night to find it at the rate they were going. Not that she blamed them. She knew they had to be very careful to preserve evidence without contaminating it.

But she wasn't going to stand around with the rest of the press corps, watching the cops dismantle the house, she decided, starting the car and speeding off down Shore Road. She had to get moving; she had to take action, even if she wasn't sure what that action would be. She figured she'd stop at the police station and see if anything was going on there. Then she'd stop in at the *Pennysaver*, where she was sure Ted was glued to the TV and listening to the scanner and probably had a better sense of the big picture than she did. She knew she was going faster than was wise on the curvy road that wound along the shore, the vast Atlantic Ocean on one side and dense piney woods on the other, but she couldn't let up on the gas pedal. It was getting darker, especially in the woods, but the sky over the water was lighter, almost lavender. It was a beautiful sight, the black water and the purple sky that was beginning to show pinpricks of starlight, but it wouldn't last. Soon night would fall, covering the town with darkness.

For a moment, she was high above the town, looking down on neat streets with rows of houses, many with lights in the windows, and then she was swooping down the hill that lead to the harbor. She was rounding the corner to turn onto Main Street when something caught her eye. A big black crow was perched on the brand-new sign pointing to Dylan's restaurant, the Irish Pub.

She braked and stared at the bird, who cocked his head, looking right back at her, first with one eye and then the other. Then he stretched his wings and flew away, cawing, right over the pub.

Lucy wasn't really superstitious, but she found herself turning the car into the parking lot, following the crow. This whole thing had started at the harbor, with the gulls and crows announcing the discovery of Old Dan's body, after all. And Toby had told her that Bill and Brian had been bothered by incidents of vandalism, which they had attributed to disgruntled Bilge patrons who didn't want to lose their favorite watering hole. But maybe something else was going on, she thought. Maybe Mikey Boy had returned to the Bilge to look for something. Something valuable, perhaps, that he believed Brigid Heaney had taken from his family and passed along to Old Dan.

She parked the car in front and stared at the door, trying to decide if she should take a closer look. Her mind was made up for her when a crow appeared, maybe the same one as before, and perched on the edge of the roof, just above the door.

She told herself she wasn't doing anything out of the ordinary as she got out of the car and approached the pub. After all, her husband was working there, and she had a definite interest in the security of the site. Nonetheless, her hands were shaking as she tentatively tried the doorknob. Much to her surprise, it turned and the door opened.

She stood there for a minute, uncertain whether it meant anything. She thought Bill usually locked up his work site, but then again, this was Tinker's Cove, where leaving the car keys in the ignition was commonplace and locking the house was such a rarity that most people had to hunt for the key when they left on vacation. On the other hand, she knew, Bill would have thought twice before leaving his expensive tools unlocked, especially down at the harbor, where someone might be tempted to "borrow" them.

She decided the sensible thing would be to give him a call and see if he was concerned about the unlocked door. So she extracted her cell phone from her bag and dialed his cell, only to be transferred to an automatic message system. She left a message but knew there was little chance he would get it; once he was home, the cell phone sat on his dresser, ignored until the next morning. She also called home, but no one picked up there, either. Where was everybody? They ought to be making supper.

There was no creak as she pulled the door open: it was brand-new and swung easily on sturdy brass hinges. Stepping inside, she reached for the light switch beside the door. Bill had installed new wiring and dimmer switches, which could be adjusted to provide bright illumination when needed for cleaning and dimmed to create a cozy atmosphere for dining. She adjusted the switch for maximum brightness and looked around.

Bill and Brian had wrought an amazing change. There was no trace of the dingy, old Bilge. The battered paneling had been replaced with clean, fresh Sheetrock, the scarred wood floor had been sanded and gleamed with a new coat of urethane, and a row of large bay windows overlooked the harbor. It was an impressive transformation.

And, more importantly, there was no sign of any intruders. She was relieved to see Bill's portable workbench standing in a corner, along with a neat row of cases containing his tools. Buckets of paint and nails and finishing compound were stacked nearby, along with a pile of wood scraps. Unused Sheetrock and lumber were propped against a wall. Bill was a neat workman and always cleaned up after a day's work, leaving everything ready for the next day.

Satisfied that nothing was amiss, Lucy turned to go. But, to her amazement, the black crow was standing in the doorway. Such encounters weren't unheard of. She'd had a similar meeting with a crow shortly after she and Bill had moved into their old farmhouse on Red Top Road. They had been using a woodstove to supplement their cranky furnace, and one summer morning she heard noises emanating from inside the cold stove. A peek revealed a crow that had somehow managed to come down the chimney and become trapped inside. Not wanting to hurt the creature, she opened a nearby window, then opened the stove door. She watched as the bird marched across the floor, as if he owned the place, then hopped up onto the windowsill and flew off. This crow, however, didn't seem interested in flying away. In fact, it didn't budge as she approached the door. She waved her hands, intending to shoo it away, but the bird had other ideas. It stretched its wings, making itself seem larger, then settled back in place, blocking the door.

"Oh, so you think you're a tough guy," she said, wagging a finger at the crow. "Well, I've got news for you." She marched over to the corner where Bill had left a broom and grabbed it, then waved it as she advanced toward the crow. The bird didn't flinch but cocked his head, fixing her with a beady black eye. It was then that she heard a whimper.

The sound electrified her. Deirdre must be here, somewhere in the building. She whirled around and began a frantic search for Deirdre. She yanked open every door; she checked the kitchen cupboards and pantry, the refrigerators, even the stove. She checked the restrooms and finally found the cellar door. Only then did she hesitate a moment before dashing down the steps, where she found herself in a dim and dank little hall with three mismatched doors. The first opened on a flight of rickety steps topped with a metal bulkhead; the second revealed the furnace. That left the third door. Taking a deep breath and steeling herself for what she might find, she opened it and discovered Deirdre, sitting alone in the cone of light produced by a single bulb, singing to herself, and playing with a pile of curly wood shavings in a cleared space, surrounded by cases of beer and liquor. She seemed unharmed but didn't react to Lucy's presence. That, and the fact that she wasn't restrained in any way, made Lucy suspect she had been drugged.

Fearing that Mikey Boy would return, Lucy grabbed her by the hands and began pulling her toward the stairs. The girl didn't resist, but she didn't cooperate, either, so Lucy knew she had no option except to carry her. She grabbed the child under the arms and hoisted her up, then started retracing her path up the stairs. She was struggling upward with her burden when she heard a voice.

"You're too damn nosey," he said.

Startled and fearing the worst, she looked up and saw the man she'd known as Paul Sullivan standing at the top of the stairs, backlit by the bright lights she'd turned on.

"I'm taking this little girl back to her mother," she said, taking one step.

"I'm afraid I can't let you do that," he said.

His tone was casual, matter-of-fact, and it terrified Lucy. She frantically ran through her options, including trying the other stairs, the ones that led to the parking lot, but remembered how rickety they'd looked. She also wasn't sure that the door to the outside was unlocked. For all she knew, it had an outside padlock, and she'd be trapped inside.

"It's time for the truth, Michael O'Donnell," she said, making the decision to stick to the path she knew, the stairs that led to the light, to safety. "The police are on to you. They're tearing the house apart. It's just a matter of time before they get you."

He laughed. "They haven't found me yet."

"Your time is running out," she said, determined not to let her voice shake. "Why make things worse for yourself?"

"At this point, nothing I do will make a bit of difference," he said, chuckling. "I'm a damned man to be sure."

"You must have had your reasons," she said, summoning her strength to climb another step. Deirdre was heavy, and she had to struggle to keep her balance and not to fall backwards.

"I only ever wanted what is rightfully mine," he said, watching her. "Brigid Heaney was a witch. She stole my father's honor and his money."

"She blackmailed him?"

"She claimed Daniel Malone was his son," he snorted. "As if my father would consort with the likes of her. A housemaid! But he paid, right up to the day he died."

"It's all in the past," she said. Lucy's arms and shoulders were burning, and her back was aching. Even worse, she was beginning to feel dizzy from the strain of holding the girl. Her position halfway up the staircase was precarious. She had to get moving or she would fall.

"In the past!" He pounded his fist on the doorjamb. "It's right here in the wood and glass and shingles and paint. And I'm going to reclaim it," he declared, hoisting a red gasoline can.

Aware it was now or never, Lucy squeezed Deirdre tighter and charged up the last few steps in a desperate attempt to escape. Thrown off balance by Deirdre's weight, she tumbled against Mikey Boy, and taken by surprise, he fell down, dropping the gas can. It tumbled noisily down the stairs, and the pungent scent told her that gasoline was spilling out. She ignored it, concentrating on getting Deirdre out of there as fast as she could. She managed to get back on her feet and struggled to disentangle Deirdre from Mikey Boy's grip. She kicked him in the head and pulled the girl by the arms and finally freed her and started toward the door, dragging the child, but Mikey Boy lunged after her, wrapping his arms around her legs and bringing her down hard on her elbows. As she fell, she screamed, "Run, Deirdre! Run!" but the girl simply stood staring at her. Then, before she knew what had happened,

Mikey Boy had flipped her over and was on top of her, holding her down by the sheer force of his weight. No matter how she struggled, she couldn't free herself. She felt his arm pressing against her neck, cutting off her breath. She tried to push his arm away with her hands, desperate for air, but she couldn't budge it. From the cellar, she heard a hissing sound, and she smelled smoke. She looked around frantically for some weapon, something to hit him with, and saw the crow, perched on the bar. It cawed once, then raised its wings as if to fly, but remained in place, growing larger and larger. The light in the room began to dim, and she knew then that there was no escape for her or Deirdre. She would die, the last of Brigid Heaney's descendants would be destroyed, and Mikey Boy would triumph.

Nevertheless, she struggled futilely until, with a squawk, the bird flew through the open door and Bill rushed in. He knocked Mikey Boy on the head with a two-by-four, grabbed Deirdre with one hand and Lucy with the other, and dragged them both through the door just as the entire place burst into flames behind them. He pushed them to the ground and crawled, pulling and dragging them, until they were clear of the fire. Turning around, Lucy saw the Bilge explode, turning the entire sky red. High in the sky, above the fire, the crow wheeled and cawed, then flew off into the darkness.

Chapter Twenty

Lucy was still feeling a bit stiff and sore when she arrived at the church hall on opening night, Saint Patrick's Day. The bruise on her neck was fading from deep purple to a bilious green-yellow, and she had covered it with foundation. As she stood in front of the bathroom mirror, applying the make-up, she had been amazed to see the bruise disappear. If only she could do the same with the memory of her encounter with Mikey Boy, she thought, but it wouldn't go away. She was still waking up in a cold sweat, terrified, from nightmares. Sometimes it was Mikey Boy pressing down on her, smothering her, and other times it was the fire, spreading its flickering tongues across the floor until it engulfed Deirdre, intent on her song and her curly wood shavings. The worst dream, however, was the one with the crow. It started out as a normal-size crow, and she tried to shoo it away, but instead of leaving, it grew larger and larger, until it spread out its enormous wings and blacked out the sky. Even knowing for a fact that Mikey Boy had died in the fire and was no longer a threat to anyone didn't help. When she woke from that dream, she was always too frightened to go back to sleep, and she'd have to creep downstairs and settle herself on the couch, with a book, for the rest of the night. That was the only way she could forget what might have happened if the cell phone hadn't beeped, announcing a voice-mail message, at the very moment Bill was returning to the bedroom to get dressed after his shower.

But nightmares were far from Lucy's thoughts as she went backstage to the dressing room. She was running through the songs, performing a silent rehearsal in her mind. Not surprisingly, other chorus members in the cramped little room were doing the same thing, and every now and then, she'd catch a snatch of a tune or notice a bit of fancy footwork as someone practiced a dance routine. Rachel was humming under her breath as she adjusted her costume, a low-necked red dress with white polka dots, puffed sleeves, and a full skirt. Lucy's costume was identical, except it was bright blue with white dots.

"Lucy!" exclaimed Rachel, giving her a big hug. "You look great!"

"So do you," she replied. Lowering her voice, she continued. "Any chance you-know-who won't be able to perform?"

"No such luck," said Rachel, with a shrug. "She looks fit as a fiddle. And Dylan's back, too. The word is he came straight from the hospital."

"He looks quite distinguished in his bandage, like a maharajah in a turban," said Pam, joining them, with her yellow polka-dot costume over her arm. She hooked the hanger on an overhead pipe and began pulling her sweater over her head. "I hear it was a near thing. He almost died at one point. They say he's made an amazing recovery."

"I can hardly believe anyone would do all those terrible things, not even Mikey Boy," said Rachel. "If it wasn't for Lucy, he would have killed little Deirde."

"It was a close thing," said Lucy, shuddering. "If Bill hadn't arrived in the nick of time, we'd both be dead."

Wiping away a tear, Rachel enfolded Lucy in a big hug. "I just keep thinking the same thing over and over," said

Pam. "Why did one brother grow up to be a murderous criminal and the other a respectable statesman?"

"Mikey Boy must have been a complete psychopath. That's the only explanation. Maybe it's genetic. Maybe he didn't get the necessary nurturing as an infant—family circumstances change from child to child, you know—but chances are, it's a combination of the two," said Rachel, who had majored in psychology.

"He had to be crazy," agreed Pam. "I mean, that collection of heads . . ."

"The police say he was under the delusion that he was some mythic Irish warrior. Apparently, it was their custom to take their vanquished enemies' heads home with them and use them for decoration around the front door," said Lucy. "The police found a notebook he'd been keeping. It was written in Gaelic and was kind of his own personal epic. He was fascinated by the old legends and got himself mixed up with a character named Fionn MacCumhaill. He thought the Malones had dishonored his father, who he believed was descended from the High Kings of Ireland.

"Dan and Dylan Malone's mother, Brigid Heaney, worked for the O'Donnell family as a maid and claimed the ambassador was Old Dan's father, and I guess it must have been true, because he paid her some money, maybe hush money. Maybe he just felt obliged to support the child. Anyway, she went back to Ireland and, with the help of her newfound wealth, convinced her old boyfriend to marry her in spite of her condition. Eventually, the boys grew up. Old Dan emigrated to America, and Dylan stayed in Ireland. When Brigid died and left them a bit of money—money that Mikey Boy claimed was rightfully his—the brothers decided to go in together and make the Bilge a proper restaurant."

"When did Mikey Boy come back to Tinker's Cove?" asked Rachel.

"The police think it was some time in the fall," replied Lucy.

"And did he plan to murder Old Dan right from the start?" asked Rachel.

"They're not sure, replied Lucy. "Maybe he just wanted to come home after being a fugitive for so many years. It could be that his mental condition had deteriorated, living all alone in that cellar with his gruesome collection of heads. . . ."

"Yeah," agreed Pam. "Winter in Maine is a bitch. Sometimes after I've been snowbound for a week or two, I'd like to go out and kill somebody, too."

They were all laughing when a burst of applause caught their attention, and they saw Dylan standing in the doorway.

"I have an announcement," he said, smiling and holding up his hand for silence. "First of all, let me say it is terrific to be back with all you wonderful, wonderful people. You've all been real troupers through this."

Despite herself, Lucy found herself beaming at him along with everybody else. You had to give it to him. The guy had something. Charisma? Whatever it was, it made him very appealing.

"Secondly, I'm afraid I have some bad news," said Dylan. Everybody groaned, fearing the show had been canceled.

"I'm afraid the lieutenant governor, Cormac O'Donnell, won't be able to attend tonight's performance as promised."

There were a few knowing chuckles.

"Apparently, he's embarked on an extended trade mission to Asia," said Dylan.

This time everybody was chuckling. "Convenient timing," whispered Lucy.

"And don't forget the cast party, after the show, in the rectory," said Dylan. "Father Ed has promised green beer for everyone. That's it. Places, everybody. Break a leg."

* * *

Applause was still ringing in Lucy's ears as she and the other cast members walked the short distance from the church hall to the rectory next door. The show had been a terrific success, capturing the audience right from the start. They'd laughed and cheered and clapped their hearts out, and it wasn't just because they were rooting for their friends and neighbors. Everyone had done a wonderful job. Each scene had unfolded without a hitch; each song and dance number had gone off beautifully. Well, there was one exception, she reminded herself. Moira had skipped her solo during the big dance number, but that was okay. Nobody in the audience caught on, and the cast members were in a forgiving mood, considering everything she'd been through. And even Lucy had to admit Moira had been enchanting on stage, revealing ability that had been hidden during rehearsals. It was as if the lights and the audience brought her out of herself and allowed her true talent to shine.

Buoyed as everyone was by the show, a few people were skeptical about holding the cast party at the rectory. "Why couldn't we go somewhere else?" muttered Tatiana. "Someplace where we could really party."

"Don't worry," advised Frank. "Father Ed knows a thing or two about having a good time."

This was met with knowing chuckles from Dave and Brian, among other members of the old Bilge crowd. Lucy found herself reminiscing, remembering when she'd spoken to them outside the closed door of the Bilge on the morning when Old Dan's headless body had been found. Back then, she hadn't suspected what strange turns her life would take in the weeks to come.

"Why so glum, Lucy?" inquired Rachel, giving her a nudge. "Are you worried about Molly?"

"A bit," admitted Lucy. Her anxiety about Molly and the baby was like the pilot light on her old gas stove; it burned constantly on a low flame, always ready to flare up into full-blown panic. "But so far, so good," she added, crossing her fingers.

"She's in good hands. They both are," said Pam as they mounted the steps and were warmly greeted by Father Ed.

"Wonderful job, everyone. Terrific show. The audience loved it. Come on in, come in, everyone," he said as they filed past.

Once inside, it was clear that Tatiana needn't have worried. The rather prim and proper parlor, where Mrs. Kelly had made sure that not a speck of dust could be found and every chair had its own lace antimacassar, had been decked out with green crepe-paper streamers and holiday cutouts. It made for some rather odd combinations, as Rachel pointed out.

"Poor St. Sebastian," she said, pointing to a sepia-tinted print that had a cardboard cutout taped over it. "You can just see his arrows poking out around that jolly little leprechaun."

"Don't worry about him," said Father Ed. "He's in heaven with all the other saints." He smiled and raised his eyes heavenward. "I think it must be rather merry up there. Practically every day a holiday, what with all the Saints' Days."

"So you think they're celebrating Saint Patrick's Day in heaven, too?" asked Lucy. The product of a rather straight-laced Protestant upbringing, she found the idea rather shocking.

"Of course, and we should follow their example. Come, everybody," he said, leading the way to the dining room.

There were oohs and aahs as the hungry cast members spied the platters of corned beef sandwiches, the bowls of chips, the green-tinted potato salad, and the huge sheet cake picturing Finian and Sharon dancing across fields of green icing beneath a colorful sugar rainbow. And on the sideboard, there were pitchers and pitchers of green beer, along with bottles of Irish whiskey and Baileys Irish Cream.

"Help yourselves," proclaimed Father Ed. "But first a toast. Get yourselves a glass, and raise it high." When everyone was ready, he continued. "Here's to our good friend Dylan Malone, miraculously preserved by heaven to direct this show, and to his beautiful and talented wife, Moira. . . ."

"Here, here," they all chimed in.

"And to the amazing Frank Cahill, who kept everyone on course . . ."

"Here, here," they repeated.

"And to all of you, who made this wonderful evening possible. S'láinte!"

"S'láinte!" they shouted, raising their glasses and downing the contents.

It was then that Lucy felt her cell phone vibrating in her pocket and, fearing the worst, withdrew to a quiet corner to take the call.

"Mom!"

As she'd feared, it was Toby. She braced herself for bad news.

"Molly's had the baby!" he crowed proudly.

"Is everything all right?" she asked.

"Everything's fine. The baby's healthy, almost five pounds, and Molly's doing great."

"Did she have a C-section?"

"No, no. She went into labor about seven, and the baby was born around nine thirty."

"That was quick," said Lucy, who had labored sixteen hours to produce Toby.

"Really? Everything was great. Just like the classes."

"Amazing," said Lucy, who, with four babies, had never had a textbook delivery.

"Well, I got a bunch of calls to make, Mom. . . ."

"Aren't you forgetting something?"

"Oh yeah. It's a boy."

"Have you named him?"

"Sure. What else? Patrick!"

"Terrific. Now we'll really have something to celebrate. Congratulations, and give my love to Molly."

Lucy closed the phone and replaced it in her pocket, then went to share the good news with Pam and Rachel, who had been hovering anxiously in the doorway.

"Is everything all right?" asked Rachel.

"You look stunned," said Pam, giving her a hug.

"That's how I feel," said Lucy. "I can't believe it. I'm way too young to be a grandmother!"

Connect with Us

Visit us online at
KensingtonBooks.com
to read more from your favorite authors, see books
by series, view reading group guides, and more.

 Join us on social media

for sneak peeks, chances to win books and prize packs,
and to share your thoughts with other readers.

facebook.com/kensingtonpublishing
twitter.com/kensingtonbooks

Tell us what you think!

To share your thoughts, submit a review,
or sign up for our eNewsletters, please visit:
KensingtonBooks.com/TellUs.